JAMES HADLEY CHASE

# Mission to Venice

**GRAFTON BOOKS**

A Division of the Collins Publishing Group

LONDON GLASGOW
TORONTO SYDNEY AUCKLAND

Grafton Books
A Division of the Collins Publishing Group
8 Grafton Street, London W1X 3LA

Published by Grafton Books 1967
Reprinted 1973, 1975, 1977 (twice), 1979 (twice),
1980 (twice), 1986

First published in Great Britain by
Robert Hale Limited 1954

Copyright © James Hadley Chase 1954

ISBN 0-586-02308-9

Printed and bound in Great Britain by
Cox & Wyman Ltd, Reading

Set in Plantin

By the same author

Don Micklem finished off the final letter and gave a sigh of huge relief.

"This sure has been a hectic two months," he admitted to his secretary, "and I'm certainly looking forward to my four lazy weeks in Venice."

Micklem would have been wiser – much wiser, had he only known it – to spend his lazy four weeks in Devon, or even no further than Brighton. . . . Because, to Venice, had come a man by the name of John Tregarth, and in that beautiful city something shocking had happened to him.

And the backwash was rolling to sweep the unexpecting Micklem under.

# Contents

# CHAPTER ONE

*S.O.S.*

---

MARIAN RIGBY, a tall, dark beauty, in a grey coat and skirt and a red fan-fronted beret, walked briskly along the carriageway of cobblestones known as Upper Brook Mews.

On either side of the mews were the garages that housed the Rolls-Royces, the Bentleys and the Daimlers whose well-to-do owners lived in the neighbouring vicinity. Above the garages were the living quarters of the chauffeurs who spent most of their spare time washing, waxing and polishing their charges.

At the far end of the mews, overshadowed by the back of the American Embassy, was a small, two-storey house. Its white face, olive-green shutters, its geranium and lobelia-filled window boxes and its gay, continental green and white sun awnings invariably attracted the attention of any passer-by.

The house was the home of Don Micklem, American millionaire, sportsman and man-about-town whose social activities were constantly reported in the gossip columns of the evening papers.

Marian Rigby was his personal secretary, and this morning she was arriving ahead of her usual time as Micklem was leaving London at midday for a month's stay at his *palazzo* in Venice.

As she paused outside the front door of No. 25a to search in her handbag for the door key, one of the chauffeurs, cleaning a mud-splashed Rolls-Royce, straightened and touched his cap.

"Morning, miss," he said cheerfully.

"Good morning, Tim," Marian replied, and her smile seemed to warm the whole mews.

The chauffeur watched her disappear into the house, and he heaved a sigh.

Marian Rigby was a great favourite of his. He saw her every morning and they always exchanged a word.

Micklem was a lucky bloke to have a girl like her to work for him, the chauffeur thought as he began to wash the car. Come to that, Micklem must have been born lucky. To have inherited five million pounds on the death of his father, to have a *palazzo* in Venice, a penthouse in New York and a villa in Nice as well as this nice little house in London was giving one man more than his fair share. But the chauffeur didn't begrudge Micklem his good fortune.

"If all Americans were like him," he thought, swishing water over a hubcap, "we wouldn't have to worry about the Russians trying to split the Western Union or whatever they're supposed to be doing. He's a toff. Always has a word to say to me when he passes. No side. That's what I can't abide about some of these rich blokes – big heads; too full of themselves to notice you, but not Mr. Micklem. Maybe he doesn't work for a living, but he's never idle. Up at half-past five this morning, riding in the Row. I've never known a bloke who sleeps so little. Blimey! If I lived like he does I'd be dead in a week." He paused to look up at the little house. "And entertain! Always some big nob calling to see him. The Home Secretary and the American Ambassador last night. A duke and an actress the night before."

He tried to imagine what he would do if he had five million pounds, was his own master and had a secretary as beautiful as Miss Rigby.

After some thought, he decided he would probably be happier as he was.

Marian Rigby took off her hat, gave herself a quick glance in the hall mirror and then walked briskly into Don Micklem's study.

It was a pleasant room, lined with books and furnished with deep, easy chairs, shaded lamps, Bukhara rugs and a big mahogany desk on which stood a typewriter and a tape recorder.

Don Micklem lolled in one of the easy chairs, a pile of letters in his lap which he was opening and glancing at with obvious impatience.

His fleshy sun-tanned face lit up when he saw her and his wide smile welcomed her.

He was a big man : close on six feet two, dark and built like a heavyweight boxer. The small Z-shaped scar on his right cheek and his black pencil-lined moustache gave him a slightly raffish air. He was wearing a nigger-brown polo sweater and tan-coloured jodhpurs. A tray containing coffee and the remains of orange juice and toast on a low table near him told her he had only just finished breakfast.

"There you are," he said, gathering up the letters and dumping them on the desk. "I was beginning to think I'd have to read these myself." He reached for a cigarette, lit it and eyed her approvingly. "You're looking very smart this morning. Is that a new costume you're wearing?"

"I wore it yesterday and the day before that," Marian said

patiently. She began to look through the letters with practised speed. "Your plane leaves at twelve. You have only two and a half hours, and there's a lot to do."

"My dear girl," Don said gently, "I am fully aware of that fact. Cherry has been driving me crazy ever since I got back from my ride. I don't know why it is but whenever I go away, you and Cherry create an atmosphere of confusion and panic. You would think I'm planning to be late the way he has been bullying me. Two and a half hours! Why Napoleon could conquer a nation in that time."

"But you are not Napoleon," Marian said crisply. "You know very well every time you go away something happens at the last moment to turn your departure into a nightmare scramble. I'm determined this time you will arrive at the airport with at least ten minutes in hand."

Don groaned.

"How pleasant it will be to get to Venice and not be bullied for a month. The fatal snag is I have to take Cherry with me." He glanced at her as she sat down at the desk and began to rip open the envelopes. "What will you do with yourself while I'm away?"

"Have a nice long rest," Marian said with feeling. "These last two months have been a little too hectic even for me."

"Yes; they have been hectic," Don said, suppressing a yawn, "but they've been fun." He got out of his chair. "I guess I'll take a shower and change. Then we'll polish off those letters. There's nothing else for me to do, is there?"

"You know very well there is," Marian said. "You have four telephone calls to make. Mr. Studleigh must have your comments on the Union Steel merger before you go. You promised that Herbert girl an introduction to Mr. Llewellyn."

"I wish you wouldn't always call her that Herbert girl," Don said. "She's a very nice little thing."

"She hasn't the brains of a louse," Marian said curtly.

"She has extraordinarily pretty legs. Old Llewellyn will be delighted with her. Besides, he hasn't any brains himself. They'll make a grand pair."

"Lady Stennham reminds you her son will be in Venice and she hopes you will see something of him," Marian said maliciously, glancing up from a letter she had just opened.

"You can tell her that if I see him first, he most certainly won't have the opportunity of seeing me. Remind Cherry to say I'm out if he calls. He's the most repulsive little worm that ever crawled out of Burke's peerage." He made for the door. "I'd better get changed. Sound's as if we've got a full day's work on our hands. Think we'll get through it in time?"

"We'll have to," Marian said ominously.

Ten minutes later, Don, now in a pale grey lounge suit, came into the study, followed by Cherry, his general factotum majordomo, valet and butler all rolled into one.

Cherry was an awe-inspiring sight. He had the stately aloofness of an Archbishop. He was tall and bulky with a pink-and-white complexion and several pink chins that quivered when he was vexed. He was of the old school. Having seen twenty years' service with the Duke of Walsingham, he knew what was right and what was wrong, and he didn't hesitate to express an opinion. He was much sought after. Many of Don's friends had tried to persuade him to leave Don and come to them, but without success. It wasn't that Cherry approved of Don, but he was fascinated by him. Even the Duke hadn't been able to offer him such a variety of visitors, such unexpected changes and such comfort. To-day he was going to Venice. At the end of the month he would be in New York. Then he would return with his master for Christmas in London, and in January he would be going to Nice. Cherry liked foreign travel. He liked to observe foreign customs and watch how the rich lived abroad. He found Don often irritating, difficult and sometimes even shocking, but he offered Cherry the opportunity to travel. His millions gave Cherry a tremendous sense of security that had been badly shaken when his late master, the aged Duke, to meet his tax demands, had been forced to admit what Cherry called "the rabble" at two shillings and sixpence a head into the sanctity of his castle. The sight of them swarming all over the place and leaving their sandwich papers on the magnificent lawns was too much for Cherry. He packed his bags and left.

"You might let Cherry have the tickets and passports," Don said, settling himself in his easy chair. "He can go on ahead and get the luggage cleared. That should save a little time."

Marian handed over the tickets and passports to Cherry who took them, an eager gleam in his bright blue eyes.

"Hello," Don said, looking out of the window. "Who's this coming?"

A taxi had pulled up outside the house, and a girl got out. While she hunted in her handbag for the fare, Don examined her critically.

"Suburban, neat, middle-class and pleasant to look at," he

murmured. "She looks as if she hasn't been sleeping well recently, and she's probably got some worry on her mind." He glanced at Marian who was regarding him with an exasperated expression. "How am I doing? Or do you think her paleness is due to pernicious anaemia?"

"I have no idea and I couldn't care less," Marian said shortly. "Will you please look at these letters?"

"She's coming here," Don said. "Now, I wonder what she wants."

"Mr. Micklem is engaged," Marian said, catching Cherry's anxious eye. "Please explain that he is going away immediately, and he won't be back until December."

"Yes, miss," Cherry said, his fat face relieved. He began to move like a galleon in full sail towards the door.

"Before you send her away, find out who she is and what she wants and tell me," Don said sharply, and there was a note in his voice that brooked no argument. "I like the look of her."

Marian and Cherry exchanged exasperated glances, then Cherry went away.

"Will you please concentrate on these letters?" Marian said. "How are we going to finish . . .?"

"Okay, okay," Don said, picking up the letters. He watched the girl come to the front door and ring the bell. Then he impatiently glanced through the letters. "Tell Terry I'll get him a chandelier if he must have one. What on earth he wants a chandelier for I can't imagine. Oh, this Sotherby woman! Tell her I'll look out for her at Florian's, but I can't manage a dinner date. Say 'no' politely to these next four, and 'no' very firmly to Mrs. Van Ryan's invitation. Say 'yes' to these three.".

Cherry tapped and entered.

"The young person is a Mrs. Tregarth. She wishes to see you on urgent, personal business," he said gloomily.

"Tregarth?" Don frowned. "I've heard that name before. Does it strike a note with you, Marian?"

"It does not," Marian said firmly. "We must get on. Here's Harry with the car."

Don glanced out of the window. His big, black Bentley was coming down the mews with Harry Mason, his chauffeur, at the wheel.

"Oh, Harry's always early," he said indifferently.

"Shall I tell Mrs. Tregarth you are engaged, sir?" Cherry asked anxiously.

"Wait a minute. Tregarth: I met a guy during the war whose

11

name was Tregarth." Don got to his feet. "He was a damned good guy. I wonder if this is his wife."

Marian and Cherry exchanged alarmed glances.

"It can't be," Marian said hurriedly. "Tregarth isn't an unusual name. She's probably after a subscription for some charity. Shall I get Mr. Studleigh on the telephone? You promised to speak to him about the merger."

"Tregarth," Don was muttering, his mind far away. "It could be. I guess I'll see her." He crossed the room with two long strides, opened the door and made for the lounge.

Marian threw down her fountain-pen in disgust.

"Oh damn and blast!" she said with unladylike vehemence. "Now we are going to be late!"

"Yes, miss," Cherry said, his pink chins quivering.

Hilda Tregarth was standing by the window as Don entered the long, narrow lounge. She turned quickly, and into her tired, anxious eyes came an expression of relief and hope.

"Thank you for seeing me, Mr. Micklem," she said. "I was told you were engaged."

"That's all right," Don said, smiling. "Come and sit down. Is your husband John Tregarth?"

"You remember him then? I was so sure you wouldn't."

"Why, sure. He's not the type you forget. I'm glad to know you. John's a terrific guy. I only met him once. That was when I took him to Rome. Those guys who dropped into enemy territory had a lot of nerve, and your husband was no exception."

She sat down.

"He often speaks of you," she said, her voice low. "He says you were the best pilot he has ever flown with."

"I'm glad he thinks so." Don was wondering why she looked so pale and ill. He could see she was tense with controlled anxiety. "What's the trouble, Mrs. Tregarth? It is trouble, isn't it?"

"Yes. I know I shouldn't have come worrying you, but I saw in the paper last night that you were going to Venice. I knew I had to come." Her voice broke and she turned her head as she fumbled in her handbag for a handkerchief.

"Now don't get upset," Don said a little startled. "Anything I can do, I'll do. Suppose you tell me what it's all about?"

She made an effort, touched her eyes with her handkerchief and turned to face him.

"John's missing, Mr. Micklem. A month ago he went to

12

Vienna. I haven't heard from him since he arrived. He – he's vanished, and I'm so worried . . ."

"Vienna? Have you reported this to the police?"

"They won't help." Her pale face was bitter. "I can't understand it. They are utterly indifferent. I've been to the Foreign Office. They won't help me either. It's as if they don't care what's happened to John." She clenched her fists. "There's something very wrong. I wanted to go to Vienna. I sent my passport in to be renewed, and it hasn't been returned. They say it's mislaid. They're watching me, too. I was even followed here."

Don had a sudden uneasy thought that this pale, scared-looking girl might be a lunatic. She was quick to see what was going through his mind by his sudden wary expression.

"I'm not mad, Mr. Micklem," she said quietly, "but I sometimes feel I shall be if someone doesn't help me." She opened her handbag and took out some papers and a photograph. "Please look at these. They should convince you I am John's wife."

Don glanced at the marriage certificate she had given him and then at the photograph. He recognized Tregarth immediately. He was with his wife, his arm around her: a puny man with a jutting chin and solemn, steady eyes.

"Thanks," Don said, and gave her back the papers. He glanced at the clock on the mantelpiece. The time was five minutes to eleven. He was supposed to be at the airport at twelve. It didn't take him long to decide that Hilda Tregarth interested him a lot more than catching a plane. After all there were other planes and other days. He couldn't turn this girl out without first hearing her story. "What makes you think I can be of any help, Mrs. Tregarth?"

"I don't know if you can help, but John seems to think you can," she returned quietly. "I received this yesterday." She took from her handbag a highly-coloured picture postcard.

He took it, frowning.

It was a picture of the Bridge of Sighs, Venice: a typical tourist's postcard. He turned it over, examined the Italian stamp and saw the postcard had been posted three days ago. The card was addressed to *Mr. Alec Howard, 133, Westbrook Drive, West Acton.* Written in a small, neat handwriting was the message:

> *Find it very hot here. Unable to get away as planned. Remember me to Don Micklem. S. O. Saville.*

Don looked up, his face bewildered.

13

"But this isn't from your husband. It's not even addressed to you."

"It's in John's handwriting," Hilda said, her voice unsteady. "Alec Howard is John's factory manager. He recognized John's handwriting and brought the card to me. Saville was John's mother's maiden name. Read the message again, Mr. Micklem. Don't you see the hidden meaning in it? People who crossed the Bridge of Sighs were condemned. He's trying to tell me he's in trouble. That's why he sent the picture. He ends his message with S.O.S. Don't you see? He is calling for your help."

Don drew in a long, deep breath. He stared at the card for a few moments. He experienced a sudden chill that crawled up his spine: a prickly, feathery sensation he used to feel during the war when he knew he was running into danger. He got to his feet.

"Wait a moment, Mrs. Tregarth. I want to hear all about this from the beginning. Please excuse me for a minute."

He went out of the room just as Cherry came down the stairs with the last of the luggage.

"I'm going to the airport now, sir," Cherry said mournfully. He gave Don a hurt, grieved look. "We have only an hour before the plane leaves."

Marian came to the study door.

"Don, please . . ." she began.

"Take all that junk upstairs again," Don said curtly, waving at the luggage. "We're not going. Marian, please cancel the tickets. Something has cropped up that I've got to look into. See if you can get reservations for to-morrow. I may be able to get away by then."

He turned and went back into the lounge.

Marian threw up her hands.

"One of these days, I'm going to . . ." She stopped short as she remembered she was setting a bad example to Cherry. "Oh well, there it is," she went on, more calmly. "You had better tell Harry."

"Yes, miss," Cherry said, in a tight, strangled voice.

She returned to the study and shut the door with an ominous click.

Cherry stood for a long moment staring at the luggage. Then he looked furtively up and down the hall and passage to make sure no one was watching. He drew back a long, bulky leg and kicked one of the handbags viciously.

14

# CHAPTER TWO

*Your Own Personal Funeral*

DON settled himself in an easy chair and nodded at Hilda Tregarth encouragingly.

"Now, let's get at it," he said. "Tell me about your husband. Take your time. There's no rush. All I know about him is that he was a saboteur during the war. The last time I saw him was when he jumped from my kite into the darkness over Rome to organize the Resistance movement at the beginning of the crack-up. What happened to him?"

"I don't know, except that he survived," Hilda said quietly. "He never talks about himself or about his war experiences. He remained in Italy a year after the war, then he came home and settled down. His father owned a small glass factory. John joined him in the business, and when his father died, John took charge. He spends three months of each year travelling on the Continent, visiting the important glass-making centres for new ideas. He always travels alone, although I would like to go with him. He left for Vienna on August Ist: nearly five weeks ago. I had a letter from him on August 6th, saying he had arrived and was staying at his usual hotel. Since then I've heard nothing from him."

"There was no hint in the letter that he was in trouble?" Don asked.

She shook her head.

"No. It was a perfectly ordinary letter. He seemed happy and eager to get to work. He said he expected to stay in Vienna a month before going on to Paris. When he didn't write the following week I was surprised, but not worried. I thought he must be very busy. My second letter to him was returned marked 'Gone away. Forwarding address not known.' Then I did begin to worry. I wrote to the Paris hotel he usually stays at, but my letter was returned. I telephoned the hotel and was told John wasn't expected there and had made no reservations. By this time, I was getting pretty frantic. I decided to fly to Vienna and make inquiries. I haven't been abroad for some time, and my passport needed renewing. I sent it in, and after waiting, I called to inquire. I was told it had been mislaid. They were very curt with me, but I didn't see anything sinister about it as I do now. I didn't know what to do. You see, Mr. Micklem, John and I are very much in love. He always writes when he is away. I began to think he might have had an accident. I went to the police."

"The local police or Scotland Yard?" Don asked.

"Oh, the local police. John is a member of the Hampden Cricket Club and the Inspector plays for the club. John and he are friendly, and the Inspector has met me and knows me. He promised to make immediate inquiries." She twisted her hands in her lap. "He was very kind. When I left I felt a lot less worried. I was sure he would do something, but he didn't. I heard nothing for two days so I went to see what was happening. The sergeant told me the Inspector was out. The atmosphere had completely changed. When I first went to the station, they were all friendly and kind. But this time I was treated like a stranger. The sergeant was almost rude. He said they had no information for me, but if they heard anything they would communicate with me."

Don crushed out his cigarette and rubbed his jaw.

"When was this?"

"Four days ago. I telephoned the Inspector the next morning, but he wouldn't speak to me. The sergeant told me it was no use worrying them. If they heard anything they would let me know. It was horrible!" She bit her lip and looked away. After a moment, she went on, her voice unsteady: "I knew then they didn't intend to do anything. So I went to Scotland Yard."

"Haven't you anyone – a relation or friend – who could have helped you?" Don asked sympathetically.

"I suppose I could have gone to my friends," she said quietly, "but I felt this was my business and no one else's. I saw someone in the Special Branch. He was very polite and distant. He told me the matter had been reported to him and inquiries were being made. He – he was almost hostile: it was the way he looked at me more than what he said. I asked him point-blank if John was in trouble with the authorities, but it was like talking to a brick wall. He said he had no information to give me, but if he heard, he would let me know. I knew I wasn't going to hear anything. I was nearly out of my mind. I went to the Foreign Office. At first they wouldn't even see me, but I refused to leave. Then some junior secretary appeared and he was hostile, too. He said it was a police matter and nothing to do with the Ministry. I was desperate by then. I made a scene.

16

I said if I didn't get some satisfaction I intended to go to the *Daily Gazette* offices and tell them the whole story."

"Good for you," Don said, immensely impressed by this tired, frightened girl's courage. "What did they say to that?"

"I might have exploded a bomb in the place. The secretary went away to consult someone, and after a long delay, I was taken to Sir Robert Graham's office. I spoke to his personal secretary. He was brutally curt. He said no one could stop me going to the *Gazette*, but if I did, I would be sorry. He was almost threatening. He said any publicity about John's disappearance would only react back on John. He told me to go home and wait. It would be dangerous to make further inquiries and I must be patient. I was so frightened I allowed him to over-awe me. I wandered about the streets for some time, wondering what I was to do. Then I became aware that I was being followed. I didn't see who was following me, but I knew instinctively that I was being followed. I took a taxi to Kensington and a black car followed me. I have its number." She paused to open her handbag and gave Don a slip of paper. "That's the number. I don't know if it can be traced."

"It's possible," Don said, taking the paper and slipping it into his pocket. "I'll see what I can do. Then what happened?"

"I left the taxi at the underground station and went home. I was followed all the way. I did see the man then. He looked like a policeman, but of course I can't be sure of that. Later, Mr. Howard, John's manager, came to see me. He brought the postcard you've seen. He didn't know what to make of it. I didn't tell him what had happened. He isn't the kind of man you can confide in. He's a very good manager, but that's all. I said John must be pulling his leg. He didn't seem to think it was much of a joke, as, of course, it wasn't. He asked if I had heard from John. I – I said I was expecting to hear from him that day, but I'm sure he didn't believe me. Then last night I read in the paper that you were going to Venice. I thought you might make some inquiries. I know it's asking a lot, but I am sure John is also asking for your help. I've got to know what's happened to him." She again clenched her fists, fighting back her tears. "I've got to know, Mr. Micklem!"

"Sure," Don said quietly. "Don't worry. I'll make some inquiries. There is one question I want to ask. Have you yourself any explanation why your husband has disappeared?"

She looked at him startled.

"Why, of course not."

"Not even a guess?"

"No."

"Forgive me asking this, you are quite sure he hasn't gone off with some woman?"

Her tired, grey eyes looked fearlessly at him.

"I know he hasn't. John isn't like that. We live for each other. It's not one of those things either of us could fake."

"Fine," Don said and lit another cigarette before asking, "Have you any reason to believe your husband is still working for M.I.5? Putting it bluntly, do you think he is an agent, or spy if you like, when he goes to the Continent?"

"I don't know," she said helplessly. "I'm beginning to think it might be possible. He would never let me go with him, and now these people are acting so strangely about him. If a spy is caught, the country employing him usually washes their hands of him, don't they?"

Don shrugged.

"That seems to be the general idea, but we don't know for certain. Now look, go home and try not to worry. Leave this to me. I have a great deal of admiration for your husband. I'll do everything I can to find him. I happen to know Sir Robert Graham pretty well. I'll see him right away. If he can't or won't tell me anything, I'll try Chief Superintendent Dicks of the Special Branch. He is also a good friend of mine. I'll find something out for you by to-night. Give me your address. I'll either telephone or come and see you."

She suddenly put her hands to her face and began to cry. Don got up and touched her shoulder lightly.

"Don't let it get you down. It's a tough break, but if it depends on me, it's going to be all right. That's a promise."

"I'm sorry," she said shakily, and touched her eyes with her handkerchief. "I don't know how to thank you. These last days have been horrible. I'm all right now."

"Go home and take it easy. I'll try not to keep you waiting any longer than I can help." He smiled at her and with an effort she smiled back. "You're not alone on this any more. Now let me have your address."

After she had gone, Don stood staring at the opposite wall, his eyes thoughtful. It looked as if Tregarth had got himself into a pretty bad mess. With the Foreign Office and the police hostile, he would have to move cautiously. He grimaced, shrugged and went quickly from the room, calling to Cherry to get the car.

Sir Robert Graham moved creakily across the hushed, sombre lounge of the Sportsman's Club to his favourite armchair in the bay window, overlooking St. James's Park.

He was tall and angular. His yellowish, thin face with its white drooping moustache, deepset, shrewd blue eyes and lantern jaw, his morning coat and high winged collar made him an impressive figure. He lowered himself carefully into the chair, stretched out his long, thin legs and nodded to the waiter who set down a glass of port on the coffee table at his side.

Across the lounge, Don waited patiently for the old man to settle himself. Sir Robert had lunched well. Don hoped he would be in a receptive mood. He waited until Sir Robert had sipped his port, then he left his chair and went over to him.

"Hello," Don said breezily. "May I join you?"

Sir Robert looked up sharply. His keen blue eyes brightened when he saw Don.

"Why, yes," he said, waving to a chair at his side. "How are you? I thought you were in Venice."

"With any luck I should be there to-morrow."

"Flying, of course. Well, well, I suppose it's all right. I must admit I don't feel safe in an aircraft. I've only been once. Didn't like it. These days everyone is trying to save time."

Don took out his cigar case.

"Try one of these. I think you'll find it better than ordinary."

Thin, yellow fingers took the offered cigar and carried it to the hooked, aristocratic nose.

"For a young man you have an uncommonly good taste in cigars," Sir Robert said. "Have a port?"

"I guess not, thank you," Don said as he lit his own cigar and blew a cloud of smoke luxuriously towards the ceiling. "How's life treating you?"

"So-so. Not as spry as I used to be. Hope to get away in a week or so for some shooting. Lord Heddisford's place. You wouldn't care to come?"

"I don't reckon to get back to London until December. I'm going to New York after Venice."

"You're going to Venice for the festival, I suppose? I hear they are doing *La Cenerentola*. Pretty thing. I heard it last year at Glyndebourne."

They talked opera for a few minutes, then Don said, "There's something you may be able to help me with, Sir Robert."

The thick, bushy eyebrows lifted.

"What is it?"

"I'm interested in John Tregarth."

Don was watching Sir Robert's face, but it told him nothing. The old man pulled at his cigar, removed it from his lips and regarded the glowing end approvingly.

"Tregarth, eh? Hm, why should he interest you?"

"I worked with him during the war. I was his pilot when he dropped into Rome in 1942," Don said. "He had lots of guts. I understand he's disappeared."

"So I hear," Sir Robert said. He reached for his port, drank a little, then shook his head. "This stuff's not what it was. In my father's day . . ."

"What's happened to him?" Don interrupted firmly.

Sir Robert blinked.

"What's that? Happened to whom?"

Don grinned at him.

"You're not going to get away with that absent-minded act, Sir Robert. Tregarth's disappeared. I want to know what's happened to him."

"I have no idea, my boy," Sir Robert returned, setting his glass down regretfully. "No idea at all. Well, I suppose I must get back to the grindstone. If I don't make a move, I won't be home before seven. Promised the wife I'd take her to the theatre to-night. Some rubbishy thing I have no doubt, but women like anything these days."

"Is he in trouble?" Don said.

Sir Robert sighed.

"What a persistent young man you are," he said. "He may be. I don't know, and quite frankly, I don't very much care." He began to pull his thin frame creakily out of the chair.

Don put his hand on his arm.

"Just a moment," he said. "I'm not going to apologize for being a damned nuisance. Tregarth's a good guy. He did a terrific job during the war. If you won't give me any information, I'll have to dig it up from somewhere else."

Sir Robert began to look a little frosty.

"Now look, my boy, let me give you some advice. This is something that doesn't concern you. Go off to Venice and enjoy yourself."

A muscle under the Z-shaped scar on Don's face twitched. It was a sign that he was getting angry.

"I intend to find Tregarth. You can either help me or I'll look elsewhere," he said, a slight rasp in his voice.

Sir Robert studied the set, determined face and saw Don meant what he said.

"I can't help you," he said quietly. "All I can tell you is that Tregarth has made a fool of himself, and no one can do anything for him. I might add he is not worth bothering about, anyway. I'm being frank with you, Micklem. I am anxious that you shouldn't go stirring things up. This is a matter of State. I can't say any more than that. I ask you not to interfere. I don't think I can put it plainer than that, can I?"

Don looked at him.

"No, but I'm not satisfied. A man who has a fine record suddenly disappears, and you don't give a damn. You've said so. I think that's pretty horrible. I have to think of Tregarth's wife. I'll be frank with you too. I think your department and the police have treated her disgracefully."

"Scarcely our fault, my boy," Sir Robert said, getting to his feet. "Tregarth should have thought of his wife before doing what he did. Good afternoon to you."

He went away, slowly and creakily, nodding his bald head as he passed to someone he knew.

Don sank back into his chair.

At least he had satisfied himself that the Foreign Office knew of Tregarth's disappearance. Sir Robert had admitted it was a State matter. *No one can do anything for him.* That was a pretty damning thing, coming from the Foreign Office.

If they can't do anything, that doesn't mean I can't, Don said to himself.

The next move would be to see Dicks of the Special Branch. It would most certainly be a waste of time, but in a case like this, every scrap of information, any unguarded word might be of assistance.

He left the club and drove over to Scotland Yard.

Chief Superintendent Tom Dicks sat behind his desk, his red, jovial face placidly contented as he puffed at his pipe.

"Thought you were in Venice, Mr. Micklem," he said. "Didn't I see something in the evening papers?"

"I got held up, but I hope to get off to-morrow," Don told him. "I haven't come up here to be sociable, Super. I want you to do me a favour."

"Only too pleased. What can I do?"

Don took the slip of paper Hilda Tregarth had given him from his pocket and pushed it across the desk.

"I want this car number traced."

Dicks looked at the slip, his eyebrows lifted and he glanced sharply at Don.

"This is one of ours. What's the idea?"

"One of your patrol cars?"

"One of the Special Branch cars."

"I see." Don had rather suspected he would hear this. "Why are your people shadowing Mrs. Tregarth?"

Dicks's face became expressionless. He removed his pipe and rubbed the hot bowl against his fleshy nose.

"If you don't mind my saying so, Mr. Micklem, I don't think that is any concern of yours."

"I think it is," Don said mildly. "Where's Tregarth?"

Dicks laid his pipe regretfully in the ash bowl on his desk.

"Why are you interested in him?"

"I worked with him during the war. His wife has been to see me. Apparently she has been here and hasn't been too well treated. I thought I might be more successful if I saw you."

Dicks shook his head.

"I'm sorry, Mr. Micklem, I can't help you. If you want any information about Tregarth, you'll have to talk to Sir Robert Graham. He's handling the matter, I believe. It's nothing to do with us."

"I see." Don tilted back his chair, his face hardening. "And yet the Ministry told Mrs. Tregarth that it was a police matter."

Dicks lifted his heavy shoulders. He looked irritatingly placid.

"He's not our pigeon, sir. You know I'd help you if I could, but he's not our pigeon."

"But aren't you looking for him?"

"I wouldn't know."

"Why are your people shadowing Mrs. Tregarth if Tregarth isn't your pigeon?"

"Are we? I don't know everything that goes on here. I have quite enough to do without checking up on what my colleagues are up to."

Don remembered what Hilda Tregarth had said. *It was like talking to a brick wall.*

"Can't you tell me anything about Tregarth off the record, Super?" he asked persuasively. "Come on; you must know something. I want to find this guy."

"I'm sorry, Mr. Micklem. I've nothing to tell you. But I'll give you a bit of advice. Keep clear of this business. It's no concern of yours, and I'm sure Sir Robert would appreciate it if you didn't take it further."

"I'm sure he would," Don said dryly and got to his feet. "Okay; sorry to have taken up your time."

"Always glad to see you, Mr. Micklem," Dicks said, rising and shaking hands. "Hope you have a nice trip."

Don drove back to 25a Upper Brook Mews, his mind busy. He had learned very little, but what he had learned intrigued him. According to Sir Robert, Tregarth had made a fool of himself and was in a mess. Sir Robert should know, but Don remembered Tregarth and doubted if he was the type to make a fool of himself. He decided to keep an open mind on this angle and wait for more information.

Why were the police shadowing Mrs. Tregarth? They knew she couldn't leave the country. Did they imagine Tregarth would return and try to see her?

Don remembered the wording of Tregarth's postcard: *Find it very hot here. Unable to get away as planned.* Was he in some mess with the Italians? It sounded as if he were in hiding or even in prison.

Again Don felt that cold, feathery chill crawl up his spine. I'm going to find him, he thought. This is right up my alley. I've been sitting around doing nothing for too long. It's time I exerted myself and went into action.

He pulled up outside his house and went in.

Marian met him in the hall.

"Now, don't nag me," he said hastily. "I've one or two things to do before I get down to work. I won't be long."

"Captain Hennessey is waiting to see you," Marian said with ominous restraint. "I told him you were out, but he insisted on waiting for you."

"What does he want? Okay. I'll see him. Where is he?"

Marian motioned towards the lounge. Don crossed the hall, opened the door and went in.

Captain Ed. Hennessey of the U.S. Army Intelligence, a big, sandy-haired man with a red, freckled face, was sitting in an armchair, glancing through the morning paper. He got to his feet and grinned when he saw Don.

"Hi, Don," he said, offering a big, hairy hand. "How are you?"

"I'm okay," Don said, shaking hands. "What do you want? I haven't seen you in months."

"This is an official visit. Why couldn't you have gone to Venice to-day instead of stirring up trouble?"

23

"Is that what I've done?" Don asked casually. "Have a drink?"

"That's a good idea. I never drink before six, but I guess my watch is slow."

As Don mixed two highballs, he said, "An official visit? What does that mean?"

"You're getting yourself mixed up in something that doesn't concern you or the United States. I've been told to warn you off."

Don gave Hennessey one of the tall, frosted glasses, then taking the other to an easy chair, he sat down.

"Is that right? Who told you to come?"

"The old man himself."

Don's eyebrows lifted.

"You mean the Ambassador?"

"Yeah. The Foreign Office has been on to him. They imagine you're going to be a nuisance. They want you to lay off."

"You're not serious, are you?" Don asked, a rasp in his voice.

Hennessey, who knew Don well, recognized the danger signal.

"Now, don't start blowing your top. We can't stop you from interfering, but we're asking you not to. This set-up could be tricky. We don't want to annoy the Foreign Office. This business is at a pretty high level."

"What are you talking about?" Don asked with a deceptive look of bewilderment on his face. "What business?"

Hennessey blinked.

"Don't you know?"

"I know a guy I once met in 1942 has disappeared and his wife has been to me to ask me to find him. What he's got to do with the Foreign Office or with the old man I wouldn't know," Don said shortly.

Hennessey scratched the back of his neck while he stared uneasily at Don.

"Sir Robert did explain to the old man, but I wasn't included in his confidence," he said. "But from what the old man told me I can make a fair guess at what's happened. This is confidential, but you might behave yourself if you know how serious it could be. It looks as if Tregarth's skipped. He's gone behind the Iron Curtain."

Don stared at him.

"Rubbish," he said curtly. "Tregarth is the owner of a small glass factory. He doesn't know anything that could possibly interest the Russians. Why should he go behind the Iron Curtain?"

24

"You may be surprised to know Tregarth was and probably still is about the smartest agent M.I.5 have got. He knows every trick in the box. He knows the names of all the agents operating in Europe and where they are. The Russians would love to have him. Now perhaps you'll appreciate why Sir Robert is laying an egg."

Don was so startled he got to his feet and began to pace up and down.

"You wouldn't be kidding?"

"No, but you've damn well got to keep this to yourself," Hennessey said.

"What makes them think he's on the other side of the Iron Curtain?"

"I'm not saying he is," Hennessey said cautiously. "It's my guess he is."

"He could have been caught?"

"Yeah, but from what the old man said I had an idea he's gone over to the other side. The old man was plenty rattled. A guy with Tregarth's experience wouldn't have been caught alive. From what I gather he is alive and talking."

Don thought of the postcard from Venice. It was on the tip of his tongue to say he knew where Tregarth was and he was certainly not behind the Iron Curtain, but an instinctive caution stopped him. He wanted more information before he gave away Tregarth's position.

"Now I've let the cat half out of the bag," Hennessey went on, "can I tell the old man you'll mind your own business?"

Don shook his head.

"No. I might not be able to keep out of it. I've promised his wife to find him."

"But that was before you knew what the set-up is," Hennessey said. "This is a tricky business, Don. We could get tough with you if we wanted to."

Don smiled.

"How tough?"

"We could take your passport away." Hennessey stood up. "It's not worth it, Don. Forget it, will you?"

"At least I'll think about it."

"Are you going to Venice for certain?"

"I'm leaving to-morrow without fail."

"Well, that's okay then. We'll take damn good care you don't get a visa for Germany. You stick to Venice and the old man will be satisfied."

Don didn't say anything.

"Sir Robert's convinced Tregarth is behind the Iron Curtain," Hennessey went on, "so if I tell the old man you're only going to Venice he can pass on the good word. Okay?"

"Sure."

"I'd better get back. Thanks for the drink. Have a good trip."

"So long, Ed."

"Just one other point," Hennessey said, pausing at the door. "If you get tempted and stick your neck out, don't go running to the Consul for protection. We're not getting mixed up in this, and if you do, it's your own personal funeral. Understand?"

"Sure," Don said indifferently. "So long."

He watched Hennessey walk along the mews towards the Embassy, then he picked up a cigarette. There was a faraway look in his eyes as he scratched the match alight.


A few minutes after six o'clock, Don stopped the Bentley outside a small villa in Newton Avenue, Hampden.

A hundred yards down the road was parked a black car in which two men were sitting. One of them half turned to watch Don cross the pavement and open the gate that led to the villa.

Don ignored him, walked up the path and rang the bell. Hilda Tregarth opened the door immediately. She looked anxiously at him as she stood aside.

"I have some news for you," Don said gently. "It's not much, but it's something."

"Please come in here," she said, opening a door that led into a small sitting-room.

Don glanced around. Although it was modestly furnished, the room was comfortable and homely.

They sat down, facing each other.

"I've seen both Sir Robert and Superintendent Dicks," he told her. "I've been wondering how much to tell you, Mrs. Tregarth. I think it's only fair to tell you the truth. You have plenty of courage, and I'm afraid you'll need it."

She sat, tense and white-faced.

"Then John is in trouble?"

"I think so. From what I've discovered, he is an agent working for M.I.5."

She closed her eyes and her hands turned into fists. Just for a moment she remained like that, then she stiffened, opened her eyes and looked at him.

"I had a feeling that was what he was doing. Has he been caught, do you think?"

Don hesitated.

"It's doubtful," he said, deciding she must be told the truth. "If he had been caught he wouldn't have sent that postcard, would he? But we mustn't overlook the fact that the postcard might be a forgery or he might have been forced to write it to put us off the track. But presuming the postcard isn't a forgery, then I think he must be still at large, probably in hiding."

"I see." She looked down at her hands. "And they're not going to do anything for him?"

"I'm afraid not."

She looked up then.

"There's something more, isn't there? Why should they be watching me? They think he's gone over to the other side, don't they?"

Don nodded.

"Yes. You know him better than anyone. Has he ever shown a sympathetic attitude towards them?"

"Never!" Her eyes flashed. "He would never go over to them!"

"From what I know of him, I'm sure you're right."

"But why do they think he has, Mr. Micklem? What proof have they got?"

"I don't know. They were pretty cagey about telling me anything. They must have a reason, of course, but only Sir Robert seems to know, and he's not talking. Frankly, I don't think I'm going to find out anything more here. My only hope of getting more information is in Venice. I leave to-morrow. I'll make inquiries as soon as I get there. Did your husband ever go to Venice on his travels?"

"Yes, he went every year. Venice is an important glass-making centre."

"Who are his contacts there? Do you know? Has he any friends who would help look for him there?"

"I don't know. He told me so little about his work. I know Manrico Rossi who owns a glass shop near the San Marco did business with him. There must be others, but he didn't mention them to me."

"Manrico Rossi?" Don made a note of the name. "Where did your husband usually stay?"

"At the Moderno. It's near the Rialto bridge."

"Have you a good photograph of him?"

"I'll get it." She left the room and in a few moments she returned with a quarter-plate photograph which she gave to Don. He examined it. Tregarth looked older in the picture than Don had imagined him to be. There were white streaks in his hair, but his eyes had the same steady determination that had impressed Don when he had met him.

He put the photograph in his wallet.

He realized the difficulty of his task. He had little information to go on. A photograph, the name of a glass seller and the name of a hotel. Hunting for a man in a tourist-packed city like Venice was taking on an almost impossible task, but he didn't say so to Hilda Tregarth.

"All right," he said. "There's just one more thing. Would you care to write a letter to your husband? If I find him, he might welcome a word from you."

For a moment he thought she was going to break down, but she quickly controlled herself.

"You are very kind, Mr. Micklem," she said, her eyes bright with tears. "You think of everything. Of course I'll write to him. Can you wait?"

"Go ahead," Don said, admiring her courage. "I'm in no rush. He may need encouragement, and you're the best person to give it to him."

She left the room. It was some twenty minutes later before she returned. She gave him a sealed envelope.

"Fine," he said, putting it in his wallet. "I'll do my best to get it to him. Now don't worry too much. You must be patient. I think it's almost certain the police will watch your mail. I'm not risking writing to you. If I have anything important to tell you I'll either fly back or get one of my friends to bring a letter to you."

"I understand," she said unsteadily.

As Don drove back to the West End, he wondered if Tregarth was thinking of his wife. He wondered, too, what Tregarth was doing at this very moment. Sir Robert had said: *No one can do anything for him. He should have thought of his wife before doing what he did.*

What had Tregarth done?

Don shook his head.

He was going to find out, and he was going to find Tregarth: not for Tregarth's sake, but for the sake of his wife.

Neither Sir Robert, the police nor Ed. Hennessey would stop him now.

28

# CHAPTER THREE

*Black and White*

---

THE late evening sun was beginning to sink behind the dome of San Maria della Salute, tingeing the oily-green water of the Grand Canal a soft rose pink as Don Micklem crossed over to the window to look down on the busy scene below.

"There's no other city in the world to touch this, Cherry," he said. "Look at that sunset. I've seen it dozens of times, but I always get a bang out of it."

"Very impressive, sir," Cherry said. "The Duke had a very fine Canaletto of this very scene. I never thought I should be so fortunate to see the original scene for myself. Most impressive."

"I guess that about describes it," Don said, picking up his cigar case, keys and wallet and putting them in his pockets. "I won't be in for dinner. If you want to go out, go out. I may be late."

"Thank you, sir," Cherry said, then coughed. "I would remind you there are several letters and invitations requiring your attention."

Don grinned.

"They can wait. I've things to do."

He left the room and went down the wide marble staircase that led to the hall.

Four years ago, Don had come to Venice for the first time and had immediately fallen in love with the floating city. He hadn't rested until he had found and bought a small Veneto-Byzantine house, known as the *Palazzo della Toletta*. It faced the Grand Canal with a magnificent view of the Isle of San Giorgio, and was a mere two hundred yards from Sansovino's masterpiece, the *Liberia Vecchia*.

Don had arrived in Venice two hours before, and now, having changed and bathed, met his Italian staff and had a word with Guiseppe, his gondolier, he was ready to begin his hunt for Tregarth.

He decided to see Manrico Rossi first in the hope that Rossi might have news of Tregarth. Failing him, he would try the Moderno Hotel.

He made his way along the crowded quay towards the *Piazza San Marco*, his eyes absorbing the bustling activities of the gondolas, the *vaporeto* steaming away towards the Lido, the barges, laden with melons and vegetables, and the *palazzo* front of marble and inlay, with their striped mooring poles.

The *Piazza San Marco* was packed with people, sitting at the tables of the cafés, shop-window gazing, feeding the pigeons or clustered in groups before the magnificent façade of the basilica with its four gilded bronze horses and its rich mosaics.

Don cut through the calle dei Fabbri. Manrico Rossi's glass shop was down a narrow alley, near the Rialto Bridge. It took Don a little time to make his way there.

The shop was at that moment recovering from an invasion of a group of tourists. They came out of the shop, sweating and tired, but determined to see everything there was to see, and Don stood aside until the last of them had gone.

He entered the long, narrow shop, and it seemed to him he had stepped into a softly-lit cave with sparkling chandeliers roofing the ceiling and the walls furnished with miracles of glittering crystal.

At the far end of the shop was a long bench at which three girls were sitting. Before each girl was a powerful gas-burner that threw a three-inch flame. The girls were holding long slender rods of coloured glass in the heat of the flame. Working with fascinating speed, they fashioned little animals by softening the tubes and bending them to shape.

Don paused to watch them work. One of the girls, a dark, thin-faced little creature, glanced up and her big eyes met his for a moment before she continued to turn the strip of white glass into a miniature, prancing horse.

He watched her set the horse aside to cool, and again she looked up at him, and he half imagined she gave him a signal; the quick lift of her eyebrows and the sudden flash that came into her eyes held his attention. Her eyes shifted back to the row of various coloured glass rods that lay before her. She took one, ran it quickly up and down in the flame, then with amazingly expert fingers she bent the rod, twisted it, bent it again and to Don's astonishment she laid before him a queer little pattern of bent glass. Looking down at it, he saw it was an intertwined monogram she had devised, and he saw the initials that stood out against the pattern she had designed were J.T.

He had scarcely time to read these initials before she had whisked up the design and had passed it through the flame, and in a moment, it had become the hind legs of yet another prancing horse.

Had he imagined it? he wondered, looking down at the sleek dark hair of the girl as she bent over her work. J.T. – John Tregarth? Had he imagined it?

"Ah, signore, I see you are interested in our work," a voice said, and turning sharply he found a tall, fat man in a grey lounge suit standing by him. The big, fat, sleepy-eyed face was typically Italian, and the smile, revealing some gold-capped teeth, was as professional as it was insincere.

"That's right," Don returned.

"It is a great honour to have you here, Signor Micklem. Four years now you have been coming to Venice, and this is the first time you have honoured my shop."

"Well, I'm here now," Don said, smiling. He had become used to the Venetians recognizing him as soon as they saw him. You can't remain an American millionaire with a *palazzo* on the Grand Canal without every trader in Venice becoming aware of the fact.

"May I show you some of my treasures, signore?"

"A friend of mine wants a chandelier. I promised to look at some."

"Ah, a chandelier! Please come to my office. I can show you many beautiful designs. Your friend would be more satisfied if he selected a special design and we made it for him. If he cares, he would be most welcome to see some of it made at our factory in Murano."

Don followed the fat man down a passage and into a small, well-furnished office. He sat down while the fat man began to look through a large portfolio full of various drawings.

"You are Manrico Rossi?" Don asked quietly.

"Yes, signore. You have been recommended to me perhaps!"

"A good friend of mine told me to come to you. A friend of yours, too, I believe."

Rossi smiled. He faced Don, a sheaf of designs in his hand.

"And his name, signore?"

"John Tregarth," Don said, his eyes on Rossi's face.

The fat man flinched. His smile became a fixed grimace. The designs slipped out of his fingers and fell to the floor. He immediately bent down to pick them up and Don lost sight of his face. Had that sudden fixed smile and that flinching look in the sleepy eyes been fear? he wondered, startled.

When Rossi straightened up, the look had gone out of his

31

eyes, although his fat face had taken on a yellowish tinge.

"Ah, il signor Tregarth," he said. "A very good friend of ours. Yes, it seems a long time since we saw him. A year perhaps or even longer."

By the way his eyes shifted, Don was certain he was lying, and he felt that feathery chill creep up his spine.

He said, "I was wondering if he happened to be in Venice. You haven't seen him then?"

"Oh no, signore." The black eyes stared at Don, then quickly shifted. The thick lips tightened. "Il signor Tregarth is not in Venice. He comes to see us always in July."

Don lifted his shoulders, then accepting the designs Rossi handed to him, he listened to Rossi eulogize their merits. He finally selected three of the more simple ones and asked Rossi to send them to Terry Ratcliffe. After Rossi had noted down the address, Don got to his feet.

"But isn't there anything I can show you for yourself, signore?" Rossi asked hopefully.

"Not right now. I'm staying a month or so. I'll be in again."

"Certainly, signore. We will always be pleased to see you."

Don walked over to the door. He paused and asked, "Has il signor Tregarth any friends in Venice, do you know?"

"Friends? Why, surely. Il signor Tregarth must have many friends here."

"Would you know any of them?"

Rossi lifted his fat shoulders regretfully.

"No, signore. Il signor Tregarth did business with me in my office. We did not meet outside."

Don nodded. As he moved along the passage with Rossi behind him, he said, "If he happens to turn up, tell him I'm here, won't you? It's a long time since we met."

"I will tell him, but I fear he won't come. Always in July he comes; never in September. Next year perhaps."

They moved into the shop and Don glanced at the thin, dark girl behind the bench who was hastily making yet another prancing horse. She didn't look up, but just for a moment her fingers faltered, and she had to discard the rod of glass she was working with.

Don paused near her.

"You work late hours here?" he said to Rossi.

"We have to, signore. The tourists expect to buy at night. We don't close until eleven-thirty."

"That's late. At that time I shall be enjoying a brandy at

Florian's," Don said, pitching his voice so the girl could hear. "Well, I'll be in again."

Without looking up the girl gave a quick little nod of her head. It could have meant something or nothing.

Don nodded to Rossi and walked out into the still, hot air of the *calle*.

He hadn't learned a great deal, but he was far from being discouraged. He had made contact. Rossi knew more than he said: that much was obvious. The girl also seemed to know something, and she was trying to be co-operative. Her mysterious secrecy bothered Don. Was Rossi in the opposite camp, if there was an opposite camp? It looked like it. Well, he had told her where she could find him and she had appeared to understand. In a little over three hours he would go to the *Piazza San Marco* and wait for her.

He decided now to call on the Moderno Hotel and see if they had any news of Tregarth.

As he walked slowly away from the glass shop, he failed to notice Rossi who was standing in his shop doorway, signal to a short, thick-set man in a black suit and black hat who lolled in a shop doorway.

The thick-set man immediately went after Don.

On the *fondamenta*, in sight of the Rialto Bridge, a tall, thin man in a white suit and white hat was staring aimlessly across the Canal. As the thick-set man passed him he jerked his thumb towards Don and nodded. The tall, thin man moved casually after Don, fifty yards or so in the rear.

Unaware that he was being followed, Don headed towards the Moderno Hotel.

At eleven thirty, Don found an empty table outside Florian's café and sat down.

The *Piazza San Marco* was still crowded. Across the way, under the shadow of the *Procuratie Vecchie* a band was playing Verdi's march of the Long Trumpets, and its robust, stirring rhythm set Don's foot tapping. Nearly every table in the vast square was taken. Groups of tourists stood about, watching the perspiring orchestra or staring up at the rich midnight blue sky, pinpointed with glittering stars.

Don ordered a brandy, lit a cigarette and stretched out his long legs.

He was no further forward in his quest. The manager at the

Moderno Hotel had no information to give him about Tregarth.

"Il signor Tregarth never comes to Venice in September," he had told Don. "Always in July. This year he does not come. Next year perhaps."

And yet Tregarth was in Venice, Don said to himself, unless the postcard was a fake, but he doubted this. If it had been a fake, why hadn't it been sent direct to Hilda Tregarth, and why had it been signed in the name of Saville?

Everything now depended on the girl from the glass shop. If she failed him, he had a problem on his hands.

He looked over the teeming *piazza*. He couldn't hope to find her in this crush. She would have to find him. He had told her he would be outside Florian's. He would have to be patient and hope she would come.

A fat man sitting at a table a few yards from him, beckoned to a waiter, paid his bill and moved away towards the basilica.

The man in the white hat came out of the shadows of the arcade and sat down at the vacant table. He ordered a brandy and opening an evening paper, he glanced casually at it.

Don remembered seeing this man as he had left the Moderno Hotel. He remembered suddenly that he had also seen him soon after he had left Rossi's shop. Now here he was again. Don's mind alerted. He turned his chair slightly so he could examine the man without being too obvious.

The man was swarthy, with a hooked nose, a thin mouth and deep-set, glittering eyes. Although he was thin, Don guessed he could be immensely strong. Steel and whalebone, Don thought, glancing at the thin brown wrists that protruded beyond the slightly frayed cuffs of the white coat.

A nasty customer, Don said to himself: vicious, and as quick as a lizard. He didn't look Italian: he was probably Egyptian.

As the man in the white hat turned his head, Don saw he was wearing gold rings in his ears.

Again Don glanced over the crowded *piazza*, then looked at his wrist watch. It was now twenty minutes to twelve. It would take the girl at least ten minutes to reach the *piazza* from the calle Formosa. He couldn't expect her much before midnight.

The man in the white hat hadn't once looked in Don's direction. He seemed completely absorbed in his newspaper, and Don began to wonder if the faint suspicion that had hold of him was a false alarm.

He happened to have seen this man three times during the

evening. Did that mean anything? Probably not, but there was no harm in keeping an eye on this swarthy-looking cut-throat.

As the two bronze giants on top of the clock tower began to hammer out twelve ringing blows on the hanging bell, Don signalled to the waiter, paid his bill and casually stood up.

The man in the white hat took no notice of him. He waved his empty glass at the waiter, calling for another brandy.

Don edged his way free of the tables and took up a position outside Florian's brightly-lit window.

The man in the white hat didn't even look to see where Don had gone, and Don's suspicions subsided.

Leaning against one of the arches on the arcade was the short, thick-set man in black. He watched Don furtively.

Don was now searching the moving mass of people in the *piazza* as they passed and repassed beneath the long row of lantern-shaped lamps.

Then he saw her.

She was looking towards him from across the *piazza* as she stood in a lighted shop doorway. She was still wearing her black working-dress, and over her head she wore a long black shawl that half hid her face, but Don was sure it was the girl from the glass shop.

He began to move slowly across the *piazza* towards her, elbowing his way through the crush. He paused once to look back at the man in the white hat who still sat at his table, half-hidden by his newspaper. He appeared to be taking no interest in Don's movements.

The short, thick-set man had also seen the girl, and he moved around the arcade, taking the longer way round, but moving faster than Don as the arcade was less crowded.

The girl waited a moment or so, then when Don was within forty yards or so of her, she turned and walked through the arch under the clock tower and into the *Merceria*.

Don went after her.

The short, thick-set man sidled just behind him.

As soon as Don had passed under the arch and out of sight, the man in the white hat got to his feet, paid the waiter and went towards the clock tower with long, twisting strides that took him quickly through the crowd.

Don could see the girl ahead of him. She kept on, not looking back, and he made no attempt to overtake her. He decided if she wanted him to catch up with her, she would have waited for him.

She kept on until she left the lighted shopping quarter and then she turned down a dimly lit *calle*. Don followed her. Halfway down, he looked back over his shoulder, but the short, thick-set man was far too great an expert in following people to be caught with his back against a light. He was waiting just out of sight, listening to Don's retreating footfalls.

The man in the white hat came up to him.

"Get around to the back of them," the short, thick-set man muttered. "Quickly!"

The man in the white hat ran down the *calle*. His long legs covered the ground silently. He darted down the *calle* that ran parallel to the one Don had just gone down.

Seeing only the empty *calle* stretching back to the lighted intersection and satisfied that no one was taking an interest in what he was doing, Don quickened his pace as the girl turned a corner.

He also turned the corner, and a few yards ahead of him, he saw her waiting for him.

"Excuse me, signore," she said as Don came up to her. "You are il signor Micklem?"

"That's right," Don said. "Who are you?"

"I am Louisa Peccati," she said breathlessly. "There is no one following you, signore?"

Don remembered the man in the white hat.

"I don't think so," he said cautiously. "Those were Tregarth's initials you showed me in the shop, weren't they?"

"Yes." She looked fearfully up and down the dark *calle*. "He is in very great danger. They are hunting for him. You must be very careful . . ."

"Who are watching him?" Don asked sharply.

She caught hold of his wrist.

"Listen!"

Don heard quick light footfalls coming down the adjacent *calle*.

"Someone's coming!" she whispered.

"It's all right," Don said quietly. "No one's going to hurt you. Where's Tregarth?"

"Go to 39, calle Mondello . . ." she began, then broke off as a thick-set, short man came rapidly down the *calle* towards them.

Don felt the girl's fingers tighten on his wrist and she crouched back. He also moved back, stepping slightly in front of her to give the approaching man room to pass.

As the man came upon them, he paused abruptly.

"Excuse me, signore," he said and waved an unlighted cigarette at Don. "May I trouble you for a light?"

"Sure," Don said, anxious to get rid of the man. He groped in his pocket for his lighter.

The short, thick-set man stepped closer. Suddenly his right fist shot up with the speed of a striking snake and slammed with paralysing force into Don's stomach.

If Don hadn't sensed the blow and tightened his stomach muscles at the moment of impact, the blow would have maimed him. As it was, the force of the punch brought him forward in helpless agony, but instinctively, he twisted sideways, avoiding the thick-set man's left that whistled up towards his jaw.

Gasping, Don threw a wild, short arm punch that caught the thick-set man under the heart, making him grunt and step back.

But the punch Don had taken had been too damaging. He felt his knees buckle. He took another punch in the body and he jack-knifed forward, dimly aware that the girl had slipped past him and was running down the *calle*.

He groped forward, trying to keep his balance. The thick-set man hit him a crushing punch on the side of his jaw. The punch didn't travel more than three inches but its impact was devastating.

A dazzling light exploded before Don's eyes. He fell face forward on to the greasy paving stones of the *calle*.

A girl's voice said anxiously, "He's not dead, is he?"

Don became aware that gentle hands were touching him and he moved, shaking his head.

"No – just knocked out," a man said.

Don opened his eyes. He could see a man bending over him: a man in evening dress.

"Don't move for a moment," the man said. "You may have broken bones."

"I'm okay," Don said. He sat up, touching his aching jaw. He could feel a slight swelling and he grimaced. "At least, I think I am." There was a dull ache in his stomach and he was thankful his hard, well-developed muscles had stood up to that vicious punch. "Give me a hand up, will you?"

He got stiffly to his feet, and for a moment, he leaned against the man in evening dress. He felt his strength flowing back, and, making an effort, he stepped away.

"I'm fine," he said, his eyes looking up and down the *calle*.

Apart from the man in evening dress and the shadowy outline of a girl in a white dinner gown, the *calle* was deserted. "Did you see anyone?"

"No. We've lost our way and came down here hoping to get to the Rialto. We nearly fell over you," the man said. "Are you sure you're all right?"

"Yes, thanks," Don said. He put his hand inside his coat. His wallet was missing. A cold, ferocious fury gripped him, but he didn't show it. What had happened to Louisa Peccati? Had she got away? What a fool he had been! He had certainly asked for it. What a sucker to have fallen for that old a-light-for-a-cigarette gag.

"Have you been robbed?" the man asked.

"I guess I have." Don was now taking more notice of the speaker. He had a slight guttural accent although his English was fluent enough. Don couldn't see much of him in the dim light, but he could see he was tall, slightly built and he appeared young.

"These damned Italians!" the man said angrily. "Let's get out of here. I'm sure you could use a drink. We're staying at the Gritti. This is my sister, Maria. I'm Carl Natzka. If you feel like taking us back to the hotel I'll offer you a good brandy."

"Oh, Carl, he must be feeling terrible," the girl said anxiously. "Don't you think he should rest a little first?"

"That's okay," Don said and he gave the girl a little bow. "Don't worry about me. I'm all right now. I'll show you where the hotel is, but please excuse me joining you. I'm in a mess and I'd rather go back to my own place. I'm Don Micklem."

"I thought I recognized you," the girl said. "You have a *palazzo* somewhere, haven't you?"

Don attempted a grin.

"It sounds grander than it is," he said. He wanted to be rid of these two. All he could think of at the moment was Louisa Peccati. What had happened to her? "I'll put you on your way."

He set off down the *calle*, and in a few moments, brought them to the lighted shopping quarter.

"You know your way now?" he said. "Straight ahead will bring you to the San Marco."

He was now able to see these two clearly, and he looked at them.

They were a handsome couple: Carl Natzka had a strong, friendly face, deeply tanned and his brown hair was bleached

38

golden by the sun. Don liked the look of him. He couldn't have been more than twenty-four or five.

His sister, Maria, was probably a year or so older than her brother. She was tall and lovely, with a determined, firm mouth, large, black sparkling eyes, thick black hair that fell to her shoulders, and her white evening dress sparkled with glittering sequins.

Don had met many lovely women in his time, but Maria Natzka had more than loveliness: she was warm, alive and exciting.

"Are you sure you won't come back to the hotel?" Natzka asked.

"No, thank you. I'll get home. Thanks for finding me."

"Perhaps we will see something of you?" Natzka said, offering his hand. "I don't like to be curious, but I must say I would like to know what happened. We won't keep you now, but please tell us some time."

"I'll tell you," Don said, shaking hands. He looked at Maria and smiled. "You will excuse me now?"

"You must be very strong and very tough, Mr. Micklem," she said, and he noticed she spoke English without a trace of an accent. "You have a bad bruise."

He grinned ruefully.

"I'm just putting on an act. As soon as I get home, I'll burst into tears. Good night."

He left them and walked quickly across the *piazza* towards the *Palazzo della Toletta*.

He went immediately to his room, stripped off his soiled clothes, and put on a pair of dark blue linen trousers, a matching shirt and a black zip wind-breaker. He changed his shoes for a pair of light, rubber-soled sneakers.

From a drawer he took a small, flat flashlight and a leather case containing a burglar's outfit. He put these two articles in his hip pockets. Then he took a roll of Italian currency from a despatch case and stowed it away in one of the pockets of the wind-breaker.

While he changed, he had been trying to make up his mind if the short, thick-set man had had anything to do with Tregarth's disappearance or whether he had been a hold-up man who had taken the opportunity of grabbing some easy money.

Don remembered what Louisa Peccati had said: *You must be very careful. He is in very great danger. They are hunting for him.*

Was the short, thick-set man one of the hunters? That was

something Don was determined now to find out.

He had had a lesson. From now on, he would be constantly on his guard. They wouldn't find him so easy to handle next time.

*39, calle Mondello.*

Was that where Tregarth was hiding? Where was it? Venice was honeycombed with hundreds of dark, badly-lit *calli*. Guiseppe, his gondolier, would know. It might be an idea to take Guiseppe along with him.

Don made for the door, then paused. He turned off the lights in the room, groped his way to the window and parted the curtains. He looked down at the quay.

Although it was getting on for a quarter to one, crowds of sightseers still moved leisurely along the quay towards the focal point of all tourists: the San Marco.

Don watched them for a few moments, then a hard little smile lit up his face.

Leaning against the balustrade, his back to the *canale di San Marco*, apparently taking his ease while he watched the crowds, was the man in the white hat.

# CHAPTER FOUR

*39, calle Mondello*

As Don walked quickly along the quay towards the *Ponte della Paglia*, out of the corner of his eye, he saw the man in the white hat push himself away from the balustrade against which he had been leaning and move after him.

Don didn't look around nor give any indication that he knew he was being followed. He kept on until he reached the gondola station.

A small group of gondoliers stood on the narrow quay where their long black gondolas were moored, gossiping and waiting hopefully to be hired.

Guiseppe saw Don coming towards him and he broke away from the group.

"You wanted me, signore?" he asked. "We are going somewhere?"

"Not in the gondola," Don said. "Come with me."

He took Guiseppe to a square just behind the gondola station where there was a small café. The two men entered and sat down at a table at the far end of the room where Don could see the door.

He ordered two *cappuccini*, offered Guiseppe a cigarette and grinned when he saw how excited and curious Guiseppe was.

Guiseppe was a famous racing gondolier. For the past three years he had won the gondoliers' race at the annual regatta, beating all comers, and he liked nothing better than to brag about his strength and his prowess as an oarsman. Tall, swarthy and immensely powerful, with a teak-hard face and heavy black moustache he made a striking picture in his black blouse and black trousers. He was on Don's pay-roll, and was much envied by his companions for having a steady income without much work.

"Do you know where calle Mondello is?" Don asked.

Guiseppe looked surprised. He nodded.

"Certainly, signore. It is near the Campo San Polo, on the other side of the Canale by the Rialto Bridge."

"That's where we're going, but before we go, there's a man we have to get rid of."

Guiseppe's eyes opened.

"We kill him, you mean, signore?" he asked, intrigued.

"No, we don't kill him, you dope," Don said shortly. Guiseppe might be the fastest gondolier in Venice, but his brain power was nothing to get excited about. "We knock him on the head. He's been following me around all the evening and it's time to discourage him."

Guiseppe eyed the bruise on Don's chin.

"Il signore has already been fighting?" he asked. When Guiseppe wasn't rowing his gondola, fighting and love-making were his favourite pastimes.

"Never mind that," Don said. He touched his jaw gingerly. "Just pay attention to what I'm saying."

"Certainly, signore," Guiseppe said, grinning. "Where is this man?"

"He's probably outside waiting for me. He is tall and thin, and is wearing a white suit and a white hat. Now, listen, here's what we do. You wait here. I will walk towards San Maria Miracoli. Give me one minute, then come after me. You should see this guy tailing me. You can't miss him. When we get to a quiet place I'll give a whistle. We'll both go for him; but watch out, he's dangerous."

"Pooph!" Guiseppe said scornfully. "I am dangerous, too. Show me this man, signore, and I will take care of him. I will hit him so, and boom! he's no more."

"Watch out he doesn't go boom first," Don said.

"I will take care of him for you, signore. It will be a pleasure. It is perhaps an affair of the heart? This man is the signorina's brother or father perhaps?"

"It's nothing of the kind," Don said shortly. He finished his coffee and stood up. "Watch out, and don't make a move until I whistle."

"Yes, signore," Guiseppe returned, looking crestfallen.

Don paid for the coffees and left the café.

He saw no sign of the man in the white hat, but he was sure he was lurking somewhere in the shadows, watching him. He set off along the dimly-lit *calle*, his ears pricked for the sound of following footsteps. After he had gone some fifty yards, he thought he could hear soft footfalls in the rear.

He kept on, not looking back, cutting down one *calle* after another.

At that hour this particular district was deserted, and when Don reached a *calle* so narrow that he could touch either wall by stretching out his arms, he gave a shrill whistle turned and quickly retraced his steps.

The man in the white hat who had been keeping just out of sight, heard Don coming back, and he, in his turn, spun around and retreated swiftly.

Guiseppe was close behind him and, invisible in his black blouse and trousers, he stepped into a doorway. As the man in the white hat passed him, he shot out his great hand, caught the man by the back of his neck and slammed his head against the wall.

Stunned, the man in the white hat sagged at the knees, and Guiseppe, still holding him by the back of his neck, turned him and hit him a crushing punch on the side of his jaw.

Don came up in time to see the man in the white hat drop like a sack of coal on to the paving stones.

"Nice work, Joe," he said, bending over the inert body.

"You see, signore, it is as I say. I go boom! and he is no more," Guiseppe said proudly and he blew on his fist. "He will sleep a long time now."

Don was going swiftly through the unconscious man's pockets. He found a short stabbing knife, but little else to interest him. There was no clue on the man to tell Don who he was.

He took out his lighter and holding the flame close to the dark, hawk-like face, he said, "Ever seen him before, Guiseppe?"

"No, signore. He is a stranger to me."

Don straightened up.

"Okay; take me to calle Mondello fast," he said.

A few minutes quick walking brought them to the Rialto Bridge. Here Don paused.

He remembered Louisa Peccati's warning to be very careful. There might be more than one man watching him. Before he went to this place, he had to be certain no one else was following him.

"You go on ahead," he said. "Go slowly and make a noise as you walk. Don't go immediately to this *calle*. I want to be sure no one else is watching us. Do you understand?"

Guiseppe nodded. This was far more interesting and exciting than rowing a gondola.

"You will be all right, signore, alone?"

There were times when Guiseppe irritated Don and this was one of them.

"Get going!" he said sharply.

Guiseppe went on ahead, crossed the bridge and disappeared into the darkness.

Don remained in the shadows. He gave Guiseppe a few moments' start, then he went after him. He could hear Guiseppe's heavy boots clumping on the paving stones. As he came onto the bridge, Don darted into one of the dark arches. There he waited, listening. Nothing happened, no one appeared.

He could now see Guiseppe on the far bank of the Canale, moving along the quay.

Still Don waited, listening. Then he heard a soft footfall. He flattened himself against the wall of the arch, knowing he would be invisible in his dark clothes. Very cautiously he peered around the arch. He saw nothing for some moments, then he caught sight of the short, thick-set man in black moving on to the bridge.

So he wasn't, after all, just a hold-up man, Don thought. It looked as if he and the man in the white hat worked together.

The thick-set man seemed uneasy. He stood in the shadow of the bridge, looking across it. Don guessed he was puzzled as to why he could only hear one set of footfalls. He probably suspected a trap. Apparently he decided he couldn't just stand and stare, and cautiously he moved forward, making no sound.

He passed the arch where Don was standing and went on until he reached the middle of the bridge. He looked back uneasily, then entered one of the arches to stare across at the far-side quay.

Don left his hiding place and ran silently up to the arch where the thick-set man stood. The man's squat, broad back was turned to him.

Like a ghost, Don crept up to him and tapped him sharply on his shoulder.

The thick-set man must have had nerves like steel. He didn't even start. He spun around and his fist struck upwards, but this time Don was ready for him. He hadn't held a brown judo belt for five years for nothing. He had hoped the thick-set man would throw a punch, and he caught his flying wrist, twisted around and pulled down hard.

With a grunt of alarm, the man sailed over Don's head and landed with a sickening thud on the paving stones. His head cracked against the low kerb and he went limp.

Don bent over him and went through his pockets. He found his own wallet stuffed in the thick-set man's hip pocket and he relieved him of it. Apart from a similar stabbing knife to the one the man in the white hat carried, there was nothing else of interest in the man's pockets.

Don left him lying in the shadow of the arches and ran swiftly across the bridge, down on to the quay and into the *calle* where Guiseppe was waiting for him.

"We're clear now," Don said. "Where's this place?"

"Down here, signore. Follow me."

Guiseppe led Don down the *calle* and into another that was so narrow the two men had to walk in single file. At the far end was a hump-shaped bridge that took them over a *rio,* down some steps into yet another *calle,* flanked either side by shabby, forlorn-looking houses that showed no lights.

"This is it, signore," Guiseppe said.

Don took out his flashlight and sent the beam on to a door just by him.

"Thirty-nine must be further along on this side," he said, keeping his voice low.

They moved forward into the darkness. A few yards on, Don paused again and turned on his light.

"This is it," he said, stepping back to look up at a narrow three-storeyed house whose peeling walls and boarded-up windows seemed to frown down at him. "It doesn't look as if anyone is living here."

"These houses are condemned, signore," Guiseppe told him. "They are going to be pulled down. You won't find anyone here."

Don was examining the door of No. 39. He noticed the hinges of the door had been recently oiled. He took hold of the door-knob, turned it and pushed.

To his surprise the door opened silently and swung inwards.

He threw the beam of his flashlight through the open doorway. The light picked up a narrow passage, a door to the right and a flight of stairs.

"Wait here," he said to Guiseppe. "I'm going in. Keep your eyes open."

"Yes, signore," Guiseppe said.

Don stepped into the passage and paused for a moment to examine the dusty floorboards. They were covered with footprints; at least one set was the prints of a woman's shoes.

He went cautiously to the door on the right, turned the handle and pushed. The door opened with a sharp, creaking sound. Don swung his light around the empty room. Dust, cobwebs and a sour, stuffy smell greeted him. A gigantic spider scuttled across the dusty floor and into a hole in the rotting floorboards.

Don closed the door and examined the stairs. Most of the

banisters had disappeared and the stairs looked old and rotten, but he could see footprints in the dust, telling him more than one person had climbed the stairs recently.

Keeping close to the peeling wall, he went up the stairs while Guiseppe watched him uneasily.

"Have a care, signore," he muttered. "Mind where you step."

Don waved him to silence, and went on up until he reached the first floor landing.

Two doors faced him.

He paused to listen, then hearing nothing, he stepped silently to the first door, gently turned the handle and eased the door open.

A sudden sound inside the room made him stiffen. There came out of the evil-smelling darkness a rustle of paper, then a soft, distinct thud.

Don snapped off his light and stepped away from the door. His heart beat a little faster as he waited, listening. More paper rustled. Then he heard a scurrying sound, and he grimaced.

Rats! he thought. A place like this must be full of them.

He put his foot against the door and gave it a quick shove, then he sent the beam of his flashlight around the room.

A monster water rat ran frantically around the room, jumped up against the wall, fell back with a thud, and scurried into the darkness unlit by Don's flashlight.

But Don scarcely paid it any attention. He shifted his light to the centre of the room.

Lying on the floor in the thick dust, the front of her black dress sodden with blood, was Louisa Peccati.

A big squat spider with long hairy legs crawled out from under a heap of rat-torn paper that at one time had peeled off the walls. Fat and obscene-looking, it moved slowly across the floor, through the pool of light from Don's torch to disappear into the shadows.

Don felt cold sweat on his face. He didn't move. He kept his flashlight directed on the dead girl. As he stared at her, he saw there was something wrong with her right hand and, peering forward, he caught his breath sharply as he saw the back of her hand was a mass of small burns as if someone had pressed lighted cigarettes into her flesh.

Suddenly coldly angry, he moved forward.

There was a flash, a scurry and a furry brown body whipped past him as the rat dashed out of the room.

Don bent over the girl and gently touched her cheek. She was still warm. She couldn't have been dead for more than half an hour, he decided.

Those two men must have caught her after knocking him out. Probably the man in the white hat had captured her as she had run down the *calle*. Don's face was hard and set. They wanted information, and they had burned it out of her. She knew Tregarth's hiding-place. She had told him to come here. The fact she was here herself and dead suggested they had forced her to talk.

He straightened up, took out his handkerchief and wiped his face.

Had these two found Tregarth?

He moved quickly out of the room, closed the door and crossed the landing to the other door. He turned the handle and pushed the door open.

As soon as he swung the beam of his flashlight around the room, he guessed he was looking at Tregarth's hiding-place.

A camp bed on which were two rough blankets, stood against the wall. A packing-case served as a table; a small box served as a chair. A half-burned candle, stuck in a wine bottle, stood on the packing case.

There was no one in the room.

Don crossed to the candle and lit it.

He stood looking round.

By the bed was a basket containing tins of food, some grapes, a bottle of wine and a long, crusty loaf. A biscuit tin contained dozens of cigarette butts, and, picking one up, Don saw it was an English brand.

In a corner lay a leather suitcase, its contents tumbled on to the dusty floor.

Don went over to it. He felt a little wave of excitement run up his spine when he saw the initials J.T. on the side of the case.

On the floor were a few handkerchiefs, a change of underwear, a hairbrush, tooth-brush and shaving kit.

Don squatted down on his heels and turned these few articles over, but they told him nothing. Obviously someone had already searched the case. If there had been anything of value or any papers in it, they had been taken.

Don straightened and once more looked around the room. Why had Tregarth hidden himself in this evil-smelling, filthy house? Who was Louisa Peccati and what was her connection with Tregarth for which she had paid so dearly? Where was Tregarth now?

Don ran his fingers through his hair in exasperation. There were so many questions and apparently no answers.

He put the various articles that lay on the floor back into the suitcase, closed it and stood up.

He didn't intend to leave the suitcase here for the police to find. If they succeeded in tracing the suitcase to Tregarth, they might jump to the conclusion that Tregarth had murdered Louisa.

Had he?

Don stiffened as the thought went through his mind. He had no proof that the thick-set man and the man in the white hat were responsible for the girl's murder. He was also jumping to conclusions. Suppose she had come here and Tregarth . . .

He shook his head.

No, he was sure Tregarth hadn't had anything to do with her death.

"Signore . . ."

Guiseppe's whisper floated up the stairs. The warning, urgent note in his voice made Don snatch up the suitcase and move quickly on to the landing.

"What is it?"

"The police are coming." Guiseppe's voice quivered with excitement. "They are already on the bridge."

Don was quick to realize his position.

There was a dead woman in the house, and she had been recently murdered. Suspicion might easily fall on him. He would have to explain what he was doing here. His explanation was bound to leak out. He might even be arrested.

"Shut and bolt the door," he said sharply, and carrying the suitcase, he went down the stairs as quickly as he dared and joined Guiseppe in the dark passage.

"There are four of them, signore," Guiseppe whispered.

A loud knock sounded on the street door.

"Come on," Don muttered and moving silently down the passage, he opened the door leading into the back room, crossed over to the window, pushed it up and leaned out.

He looked down at the dark, oily water a few feet below the level of the window.

A violent sound of splintering wood told him the police were forcing the street door.

48

"Can you swim, Joe?" he asked as he swung his leg over the window sill.

"Yes, signore."

"You'd better be good," Don said. "I've got this suitcase. You'll have to tow me. Come on."

He slid down into the water, turned on his back, holding the case across his chest.

Guiseppe joined him in the water. Don reached out and took a hold of Guiseppe's blouse.

"Get me out of here," Don said, "and hurry."

With long, powerful strokes, Guiseppe swam into the darkness, pulling Don after him.

When they were clear of the house, Guiseppe headed for the quay. While Don trod water, Guiseppe hauled himself up, then bent and took the suitcase from Don as Don struggled on to the quay.

"I hope you are enjoying yourself," Don said, grinning.

Water dripped from him, making puddles at his feet. He took the suitcase, also dripping water, from Guiseppe.

"Let's get home. I've had about enough for to-night."

They walked quickly and silently through the maze of dark *calli*.

The San Marco clock was striking three o'clock as they crossed the Grand Canale by the *Ponte dell'Accademia*.

At this hour the far side quay was deserted, and no one saw them as they walked quickly towards the *Palazzo della Toletta*.

At the lighted entrance, Don paused.

"Get off home," he said to Guiseppe. "Come and see me to-morrow. Thanks for your help."

"I've enjoyed myself," Guiseppe said simply.

"There's one more thing you can do for me," Don went on. "See if you can get any information for me about a girl who calls herself Louisa Peccati. I want to find out where she lives, if she has any people. She works at Rossi's glass shop. Be careful who you ask. The police are interested in her."

"Yes, signore. I will find something for you by to-morrow."

"Good night, Joe, and thanks again," Don said.

As he entered the hall, he saw Cherry sitting on one of the massive hall chairs. He was dozing, an expression of stern disapproval on his pink and white face.

As Don closed the front door, Cherry started and opened his eyes.

"Mr. Micklem!" he gasped. "You're wet!"

"So I am," Don said cheerfully. "What are you doing out of bed at this hour?"

"I was waiting up for you, sir," Cherry said, getting to his feet. "Have you had an accident?"

"Nothing like that. I just fancied a swim. Get off to bed."

"I'll come up and take your wet clothes," Cherry said frostily.

"Go to bed! I'll leave them in the bathroom. Good night, Cherry," and Don went up the stairs, leaving a trail of drips behind him.

He entered his bedroom, closed the door, set the wet suitcase down in a corner, then crossed to the bathroom. He stripped off his wet clothes, took a shower, put on a pair of pyjamas and returned to his bedroom.

He sat on the edge of his bed, lit a cigarette and stared down at the floor.

He rubbed his aching jaw as he considered the events of the evening.

Not a very successful effort, he thought, frowning. Plenty has happened, but I've got nowhere. I'm just as far from finding Tregarth as I was when I arrived this afternoon. But at least I do know he's somewhere in Venice or at least he was here recently.

Is he still here? Is he still alive? Did those two guys catch him and if they did, did they treat him as they treated the girl?

How was it the police turned up as they did? If I had been caught in that house, it would have been damned awkward. Was that the idea? Had there been a third watcher, and when he saw me go to the house, had he tipped the police?

Don shook his head.

I've got to get some sleep, he told himself, stubbing out his cigarette. He rolled into bed. Right now it looks as if I'm up against a blank wall. There are no more leads to follow unless Guiseppe finds out something about the girl that'll give me an idea to work on.

He closed his eyes.

But sleep didn't come easily. His mind was haunted by the image of Louisa Peccati's tortured body. Finally, when he did drift into sleep, it wasn't the murdered girl who came into his uneasy dreams, but the dark, lovely Maria Natzka.

# CHAPTER FIVE

*The Voice from Paris*

---

IT was after eleven o'clock the following morning before Don had finished attending to his more urgent correspondence, answering a number of telephone calls from people who had heard he had arrived in Venice, and had made his excuses for unaccepted invitations.

He was inclined to be curt with the last caller, and when he had hung up, he told Cherry to put no more calls through to him.

"I haven't time for social activities this trip," he said. "Tell them I've got measles or something if they keep pestering."

Cherry looked at him in alarm.

"I beg your pardon, sir?"

"I have an important job to do," Don said patiently. "I'm not being sociable for some time."

"Am I to understand, sir," Cherry said, drawing himself up to his full majestic height, "that you will not be entertaining now you are here?"

Don knew how much Cherry had been looking forward to organizing parties and dinners, and he felt a little guilty as he avoided Cherry's accusing eyes.

"That's the idea," he said, sweeping a pile of answered letters into his wastepaper basket. "I've got to find a man who's got himself lost. It's a matter of life and death, Cherry. Sorry, but it's just one of those things."

"I see, sir," Cherry said frostily. "Something to do with the young person's visit before we left London no doubt."

"Right first time," Don said. "I have to go out. Now, relax, Cherry. You're on vacation. Go and look at some pictures or paddle in the lagoon. Take your hair down and have a good time."

He hurried from the room before Cherry could recover his breath, and leaving the *palazzo*, he walked briskly along the quay towards the gondola station.

He hoped by now Guiseppe might have some information for him, but there was no sign of him when Don reached the station. A gondolier, lounging in the sun, told him he hadn't seen Guiseppe as yet.

Too early, Don thought, as he walked to the edge of the quay to look across the expanse of blue water while he decided what he was going to do.

"It's Mr. Micklem, isn't it?" a girl's voice said.

Turning, he found himself looking into the sparkling, dark eyes of Maria Natzka.

He thought she looked enchanting in her pale blue frock and big picture hat.

"Why, hello," he said, taking off his hat. "How nice to see you again."

"How is your bruise?"

"It's fine, thank you. My jaw's a little stiff, but it doesn't stop me talking."

He thought she was quite the loveliest woman he had ever met, and the Tregarth problem faded into the background of his mind as he looked at her.

"We were very worried about you," Maria said. "I told Carl he should have seen you home."

Don laughed.

"You don't have to worry about me. I thrive on rough treatment. What are you doing here this morning?"

"I was planning to see the Colleoni statue. Can you tell me where I can find it?"

"You had best go by gondola. It's by the church of Santi Giovanni e Paolo which is also worth looking at. The church is a kind of Pantheon of the Doges."

Seeing the interest in her sparkling eyes, and slightly intoxicated by her ravishing smile, he went on before he could stop himself: "You may not think so to look at me, but I'm an expert guide. Would you like me to take you and fill in the background or would you rather go alone?"

"I'm going to be quite brazen and admit I was hoping you would offer," she said and laughed. "The last time I ventured alone in a gondola, the wretched man ran after me all the way to the hotel, insisting I hadn't paid him enough."

"It's a favourite dodge of theirs. You have to know how to handle them. Come with me. I'll show you how it's done."

She moved with him towards the gondola station. She had the easy, graceful carriage of a mannequin, and Don noticed how a group of young American tourists stared at her and then at him.

One of the gondoliers came forward, bowing.

"Il Campo dei Santi Giovanni e Paolo," Don said to him as he helped Maria into the gondola.

He sat beside her and stretched out his long legs. At the back of his mind, he knew he shouldn't be doing this. He should be trying to find Tregarth, but the temptation to share the company of this enchantress was too much for him. He tried to console his conscience by telling himself he had nothing to work on until Guiseppe reported to him and he was entitled to an hour or so to himself.

"Where's your brother this morning?" he asked. "Why isn't he looking after you or has he found someone else's sister to look after?"

"He is working this morning. You see, I am on holiday, but he is here on business."

"Are you staying long?" Don asked.

"Perhaps a week. It depends on Carl. You are very fortunate, Mr. Micklem, to be your own master."

"Don, perhaps, would be less formal," Don said. "Could we make it Don?"

She looked at him from under her long eyelashes.

"If it would please you."

"It would. To return to your remark. I guess I am lucky," Don said. "Your brother said your name was Maria: it is a lovely name. What about you? Have you been lucky, Maria?"

She lifted her elegant shoulders.

"Not always. I am more lucky than some, less lucky than others. My father had a very bad time during the war. He was in a concentration camp. Carl and I were refugees. When the war was over, my father rebuilt his business. Then perhaps you could say I became lucky. I was able to have many things I couldn't have when I was a child. It would have been better, I think, if I could have had those things when I was a child. I missed them so much then, whereas now, I don't think I would have missed them."

"Your father is still alive?"

"Oh yes, but he sends Carl to buy glass. He is more interested in the financial side of the business."

"Glass? Is that Carl's job?"

Don's mind alerted.

She looked at him, smiling.

"You sound surprised. The Natzka glass factory is well-known."

A cold, feathery feeling crawled up Don's spine.

"I must confess my ignorance. Your brother then is here to buy Venetian glass?"

"Yes. We have thirty shops in Hungary. We sell a lot of Venetian glass."

"Do you sell English glass too?"

"Yes, a lot of it, and even a little American glass as well," she said, smiling.

Don tried to sound casual, but he found himself strangely tense with excitement.

"Who do you deal with in England?" he asked.

"With John Tregarth of Hampden," she said without hesitation. "And in America with the Van Ryder factory. You see, I know quite a lot about the business although Carl tries to make out I don't take any interest in it."

At this moment the gondola swung to the quay and the gondolier sprang from the gondola and held it steady.

"Well, here we are," Don said, glad of the respite so he could consider what his next move should be. He helped Maria to alight. "Wait for us," he said to the gondolier and, together, they walked across the *campo* and stood under the statue of Colleoni.

Don had taken many of his friends to see the statue and he knew its history well. He told Maria who Colleoni was, and how Verrocchio, the master of Leonardo da Vinci, had designed the statue which was considered to be the finest equestrian statue in the world.

"There's only one other equestrian statue that can compete with this one," he concluded, "and that is Donatello's Gattamelata in Padua."

While he talked his mind was seething with suppressed excitement. Had it been a coincidence that Tregarth's name had cropped up as it had done or was she connected in some way with this affair?

He decided not to appear anxious for information about Tregarth, and having explained the history of the Colleoni statue, he took her into the church and gave her a brief description of the various Doges' tombs.

When he felt she had seen enough of the wonders of the church, he suggested they should return to the gondola.

"It's getting hot now," he said. "The best place in the Venetian heat is on the water. Let's take a tour through the *rii* and talk."

"Are you sure you can spare the time?" she asked, and he could see she was teasing him.

"I'm not considering myself," Don said, grinning. "The gondolier expects it of us and I wouldn't like to hurt his feelings."

She followed him out into the blinding sunshine.

When they had once more settled in the gondola, and the long, black boat was moving effortlessly through the still water of the *rio*, Don said, "You mentioned John Tregarth just now. Do you know him?"

"Know John? Why, of course. He is an old friend of ours. Why do you ask?"

"I used to know him. I haven't seen him for a long time now: not since the war."

She half turned to look at him.

"You couldn't be the American pilot he has often talked about. You must be! How stupid of me. I didn't associate you with the Don Micklem John admires so much. You took him to Rome during the war, didn't you?"

"That's right. Have you seen him recently?"

"He was here three days ago," Maria said and her eyes darkened, losing their sparkle. "Both Carl and I are very worried about him. We think he is in some kind of trouble."

"Trouble? Why do you say that?"

"He left so hurriedly. He seemed so upset."

"Then he has left Venice?"

"Oh yes. He left for Paris three nights ago."

A barge, laden with empty chianti bottles, came slowly down the *rio*, poled by two ragged young boatmen.

Muttering in disgust, Don's gondolier edged his boat against the wall of a house to let the barge through. There was an exchange of insults as the barge passed, but Don wasn't ever aware that the gondola had stopped.

*He left for Paris three nights ago.*

This information startled him. If it were true, then he was wasting his time running around Venice hunting for Tregarth. But was it true? Had she been misinformed? Was she lying?

"That's disappointing," he said casually. "I should like to have met him again."

"We are very fond of John," Maria said. "I wish I knew what was the matter. He went off in such a hurry: it was almost as if he was running away from someone. Carl says I'm imagin-

55

ing it, but I'm sure I'm not. John wasn't only worried, he seemed frightened."

"Are you sure he went to Paris?"

"Yes. We saw him on the train."

"When you said just now he seemed frightened, didn't you ask him what was bothering him?"

She nodded.

"He wouldn't say. 'It's something I can't discuss,' he said. 'You two have got to keep out of it. It will be all right when I get to Paris.' Those were his exact words. He asked us to go with him to the station. We were going to a party and Carl said there wasn't time. John got very agitated. He said we must come to the station with him. I had an idea he was nervous of going alone. He was so insistent that we did go with him." She shook her head. "I don't know what to make of the whole thing. It's been worrying me."

"Sounds odd," Don said, puzzled. "How long was he in Venice?"

"He was here when we arrived. I think he was here for about five days. And that's another thing that puzzles me: Carl and he more or less cover the same ground. None of the people Carl has been to see have seen John. He couldn't have done any work here."

"Do you know where he is staying in Paris?"

"The Chatham Hotel. We asked him to write, but he hasn't. We shall be going to Paris as soon as Carl has completed his business here. We hope to see something of him then. I will tell him I met you. I know he will be disappointed he missed seeing you."

"I'm sorry, too," Don said. He wondered if he should tell Maria what he knew about Tregarth, but decided not to. "Did he visit your factory before coming to Venice?"

She shook her head.

"He usually does, and when he does, he stays with us, but this trip, he wrote to say he wasn't coming so far, and he hoped he would see us in Venice."

"Did he seem worried when you first met him here or did the worry develop later?"

"It developed later. He was at the station to meet us and he seemed in good spirits then. We thought he would be staying at the Gritti where Carl always stays, but he said he was staying with friends. He didn't say who they were. We all had dinner together, and we arranged to meet the next morning. Something must have happened during that night and the following day. He didn't meet us, but just as we were leaving for the party, he came to the hotel. He said he was leaving for Paris immediately and would we go with him to the station. It was then we both saw how agitated he was."

"And you haven't heard from him since?"

"No."

"How do you know he is staying at the Chatham Hotel? Did he tell you that was where he intended to stay?"

"Yes. He said he would probably be in Paris for ten days, and would we join him at the Chatham when Carl had completed his business here."

"Well, I shouldn't worry about him," Don said, smiling. "He'll probably tell you about it when next you meet."

"I hope so," she said seriously. "We are both very fond of him and it worries us."

Don turned the subject. He began to point out the various places of interest as the gondola drifted through the *rii*, but his mind was busy as he talked.

It would be easy enough to find out if Tregarth was at the Chatham Hotel. What if he were? Don didn't relish a journey to Paris, but he had Hilda Tregarth's letter to deliver and if Tregarth was in Paris, he would have to make the journey. But was he? If he had left Venice as Maria said he had, why all the excitement the previous night? Why had Don been followed? Why had Louisa Peccati been murdered?

The only explanation Don could think of was that Tregarth had found he had to drop out of sight. He had told Maria and Carl he was going to Paris and had taken them with him to guard against attack. He had boarded the train, but had got off at the next station, returned to Venice and had hidden himself in that broken-down house in calle Mondello. In this way, he had hoped to shake off his watchers – probably the thick-set man and the man in the white hat. But they hadn't been fooled. They had found out Louisa Peccati knew where he was, tortured her until she told them, and then had gone to 39, calle Mondello. Had they found him or had he escaped again? Was that the explanation?

"Will you come back to the hotel and lunch with us?" Maria asked, breaking in on his thoughts.

As much as Don would have liked to accept the invitation, he knew he couldn't waste any more time. He had a lead and he had to follow it up. Besides, it was probable Guiseppe had news for him.

"I'd like to very much, but unfortunately I have a lunch date." He looked at his wrist watch. "I'll have to get back now, if I'm not going to be late."

"Perhaps to-morrow, then?" she said. "I've so enjoyed my morning."

"I'll give you a call at the hotel," Don said, knowing it was unlikely he would have the time to keep a date with her.

They walked together to the *Gritti Palazzo*.

"Thank you, Don, for giving me such an interesting morning," Maria said as they paused outside the hotel. "I will recommend you to all my friends as a learned and expert guide."

Don grinned.

"I have no intention of recommending you to my friends as an enchanting and lovely companion. Competition must be keen enough without advertising."

She gave him her slim, cool hand, then smiling she went into the hotel.

As Don moved towards the *Palazzo della Toletta*, he found himself regretting parting with her, but as soon as he saw Guiseppe waiting for him on the steps of the *palazzo*, he dismissed her from his mind.

"Come in," he said to Guiseppe and led the way to his study. He poured a glass of wine for Guiseppe, then asked, "Any news? Did you find out anything about the girl?"

"Yes, signore," Guiseppe said gravely. "Did you know she was murdered last night?"

Don nodded.

"Yes. Did you find out where she lives?"

"She lives with her father on the Fondamente Nuove. They have a little house next to Luigi's restaurant."

"Does her father know yet that she is dead?"

"Yes, signore. It has been a very great shock to him. He is old and ill. At one time he used to be a guide, but he had an accident and lost both legs. The girl kept him and herself on what she made at Rossi's glass shop. You know Rossi's glass shop, signore?"

Again Don nodded.

"The police have seen the old man?"

"They were there this morning."

"Okay. You say he lives next door to Luigi's restaurant? Where exactly is that?"

"By the Rio di Panada. If you wish to go there, signore, I will take you."

Don looked at his watch. The time was a few minutes after one o'clock.

"Be here at half past two. We'll go together."

"Yes signore."

When Guiseppe had gone, Don rang for Cherry.

Cherry entered, his pink-and-white face displaying frosty dignity.

"You rang, sir?"

"I want lunch in twenty minutes. Bring me a large dry martini, and stop looking as if you've swallowed a fish hook," Don said, grinning.

Cherry lifted his eyebrows and refused to come off his high horse. He had been thwarted and he was determined to underline the fact.

"Very good, sir," he said and walked out, his back as stiff as a ramrod.

Cherry's airs and graces never had any effect on Don, but Cherry never gave up trying.

Don reached for the telephone and lifted the receiver.

"Get me the Chatham Hotel, Paris, right away," he said to the operator.

"I will call you back, signore."

Don hung up, lit a cigarette and began to pace slowly up and down. He scarcely noticed Cherry enter and place the cocktail on the desk.

"Excuse me, sir," Cherry said stiffly. "Lady Denning telephoned. She is giving a small dinner after the opera to-night and hopes you will join her."

"Call her up and say I have a previous appointment," Don said. "I thought I told you I'm not accepting any invitations this trip?"

Cherry stiffened.

"May I remind you, sir, you have a duty to your friends? This house, sir, up to now, has played an important part in the success of the season. I may say our dinner parties are famous . . ."

"I'm sorry, Cherry, but there are more important things to do this trip than throw parties. Now be a good guy and don't worry me," Don said.

"Very good, sir," Cherry said, his pink chins trembling. He walked majestically to the door, closing it with an ominous little click.

"Don shrugged, drank half the cocktail, then set the glass down hurriedly as the telephone bell rang.

"Your call to Paris, signore."

"Thank you. Hello, is that the Chatham Hotel?" Don asked.

"Yes, monsieur. The reception desk here," a smooth voice said in English.

"Have you a Mr. Tregarth staying with you? Mr. John Tregarth?"

"If you will hold on a moment, please."

Don stubbed out his half-smoked cigarette and drummed on the desk with impatient finger-tips.

"Hello, monsieur? Yes, Mr. Tregarth is staying with us."

Don drew in a long, slow breath. He realized then that he hadn't believed Maria's story that Tregarth had left Venice. He had expected the reception clerk to tell him Tregarth was not known at the hotel.

"Is he in?"

"I believe so, monsieur. Shall I inquire?"

"This is Mr. Don Micklem calling. Will you put me through to his room?"

"One moment, monsieur."

There was a long pause, then Don heard a sharp click on the line and a voice said, "Hello? This is John Tregarth speaking."

It was nearly thirteen years since Don had met and talked with Tregarth, and most of their conversation had been carried on against the roar of four aircraft engines as they flew from a Middle East airfield towards Rome. He had no hope of remembering what Tregarth's voice sounded like. This thin, far away voice he was listening to now could have been Tregarth's voice; it could have been anyone's voice.

"This is Don Micklem," Don said. "Do you remember me, John?"

There was a pause, then the voice said, "Yes, I remember you."

Don found himself pressing the receiver close to his ear so as not to miss any word or inflexion that might come over the line.

"How are you, John? It's a long time since we met, isn't it?"

"I suppose it is. Time doesn't mean much to me," the voice said. "Where are you?"

There was something about the voice that made Don uneasy; it didn't sound quite human. It was as if he were listening to a lifeless, spirit voice; a voice that had no body.

"I'm in Venice," he said. "John, I have a letter for you from your wife. She's worried about you."

"Worried? Why?"

The flat, mechanical voice began to get on Don's nerves.

"My dear man," he said sharply, "she hasn't heard from you for six weeks. Of course she's worried. What have you been up to?"

There was a long, empty pause. Don listened to the faint hum that came over the line. He wondered if he were imagining the sound of quick breathing that seemed to beat against his ear.

"Hello? Are you there, John?"

"Yes," the flat, lifeless voice said. "What were you saying?"

"Your wife hasn't heard from you for six weeks. What have you been up to?" Don repeated, raising his voice.

"Six weeks?" The voice went up a note. "It can't be as long as that. I wrote to her. I know I did."

"She has had only one letter from you and that was six weeks ago," Don said. "What have you been up to, John?"

"Six weeks . . ."

The voice died away and there was silence on the line, then as Don was about to speak he heard a faint sound that sent a chill crawling up his spine: the strangled sound of a man weeping.

"John!" Don said sharply. "What's the matter? Are you ill?"

Again there was a long pause, then the voice said tonelessly, "I don't know. I think I must be going mad. I don't know why I'm here. I don't know what I'm doing. For God's sake, Micklem, come and help me."

"Take it easy," Don said, shocked. "I'll come right away. Stay where you are. I'll get a plane from the Lido and I'll fly straight to Paris. I'll be with you in four or five hours at the latest. Just stay where you are, and take it easy."

"Hurry . . ." the voice moaned. "Please hurry . . ."

It was just a shade overdone. Just enough to make Don suddenly suspicious.

"I'm coming now," Don said, his eyes alert, his mouth a hard line. "Just take it easy. So long for now."

He flicked his finger-nail sharply against the mouthpiece of the telephone in the hope that the man at the other end of the line would think he was hearing the connection breaking.

Don continued to hold the receiver against his ear while he listened, straining every nerve to catch the slightest sound.

The ruse worked.

He heard a faint laugh. A far-away voice of a man speaking as if he were some feet from the telephone said: "He swallowed it hook, line and sinker."

Another man's voice snapped: "Shut up, you damned fool . . ." and the line went dead.

# CHAPTER SIX

*Counter-Punch*

---

FOR a long moment Don sat staring at the opposite wall, his mind busy. He wasn't often angry, but now his temper was at boiling-point. He had very nearly been made a fool of, and that hurt his pride. If the man at the end of the line hadn't slightly overplayed his part, Don would have rushed off to Paris. Now that he knew it was a trick, he saw clearly that whoever was behind Tregarth's disappearance was anxious to get him out of Venice.

What annoyed him even more was being taken in by Maria Natzka.

You certainly fell for her, he thought, banging his fist on his desk. She and her brother must be mixed up in this and you should have suspected her the moment she claimed to know Tregarth. Okay, it was smoothly done, but you should have been suspicious. That's what comes of falling for a pair of sparkling eyes.

At least, he consoled himself, he hadn't given anything away. He had merely claimed to be an old friend of Tregarth's.

Cherry came in at this moment.

"Lunch is served, sir," he said coldly.

Don went into the dining-room and sat down at the table. He made a hurried meal scandalizing Cherry by refusing most of the courses. While he was eating, his mind was busy, and by the time he had finished he had a plan of action ready.

"Go and have your lunch," he said to Cherry as he pushed back his chair and stood up. "Then come and see me. There's something I want to talk to you about."

Cherry raised his eyebrows. If Mr. Micklem thought he could talk him into accepting a partyless season at the *palazzo,* he was making a grave mistake, he told himself.

"Very good, sir," he said stiffly.

"And hurry: don't be longer than ten minutes. This is urgent," Don said and went back to his study.

He picked up the telephone and called the *Gritti Palazzo.*

"May I speak to la signorina Natzka?" he said when he got through to the reception desk. "This is Mr. Micklem calling."

"If you will hold on a moment, please, signore."

There was a little delay, then Maria's voice came over the line.

"Hello, Don. I'm sorry to have kept you waiting. I was in the restaurant."

"I hope I haven't interrupted your lunch," Don said, "but I wanted to speak to you. When I got back here, I called the Chatham Hotel and spoke to Tregarth. I had a very disturbing conversation with him. He asked me to go and see him right away."

"Isn't he well?" she asked anxiously, and if Don hadn't been sure she was in the plot to get him to leave Venice, he would have been completely taken in by the alarm in her voice.

"I don't think he can be. I couldn't get much out of him, but it looks as if he's gone a little crazy. He's certainly in the middle of a nervous breakdown. He was crying and hysterical and didn't seem to know what he was doing."

"This is dreadful!" Maria exclaimed. "Hasn't he anyone to look after him?"

"He seems to be quite alone. He begged me to go to him, and I'm going. I'll charter an air-taxi from the Lido. I should reach Paris in about four or five hours. I was wondering if you would like to come with me. A woman's sympathy would be helpful as he is so hysterical."

There was a slight pause, and Don showed his teeth in a hard, mirthless smile. What excuse would she make? he wondered. If he hadn't been sure she would refuse to go with him, he wouldn't have asked her.

"I'm afraid I can't possibly get away to-day," she said at last. "I don't think I can get away to-morrow either. You see, Carl is giving an important business party and I have to be his hostess."

"Sure, I thought maybe you'd be tied up, but if you had been able to get away, I think it would have been a good idea for you to see him. I'll talk to him, and if he is as bad as I think he is, I'll take him home. I'll be out here again by the end of the week."

"I think it is very good of you to break up your holiday like this," she said. "I only wish I could do something. I'll tell Carl at once. If he thinks he can get away earlier, shall we come to Paris? Would you like us to?"

"Unless you can come to-day, I don't think it matters," Don said. "If he really is bad I intend to fly him home to-night."

"Perhaps that would be the best thing. Please let me know what happens. We will be here for another four days, and after that we shall be at the Chatham Hotel."

"I should be back here within two or three days. I'll see you before you leave for Paris. I must hurry. I have some packing to do and then I've got to get to the airport. Goodbye now."

"Goodbye, Don." The inflexion in her voice was well done. "I do think it is splendid of you."

"Oh, nonsense," Don said. "I'll be seeing you soon," and he hung up.

You'll be seeing me a damn sight sooner than you expect, my clever little schemer, he thought, and that also goes for your handsome brother.

Cherry rapped on the door and entered.

"Come in, Cherry, I have a job for you," Don said. "Shut the door and sit down."

"I beg your pardon, sir!" Cherry said, scandalized.

"Oh, sit down!" Don snapped impatiently. "This is no time to stand on ceremony. I've a lot to say to you and you've got to conserve your energies. Sit down, man!"

Slowly and frostily, Cherry lowered his bulk to rest on the edge of the most uncomfortable chair in the room. He somehow managed to give the impression that he was still standing.

Rapidly, Don gave him a brief account of Hilda Tregarth's visit, her request for help, his meeting with Sir Robert Graham and Superintendent Dicks. As he talked Cherry began to relax, and his forbidding expression faded to one of interest. By the time Don had told him of his meeting with Rossi, his encounters with the thick-set man and the man in the white hat and the finding of Louisa Peccati's body, Cherry's eyes were popping and he had completely forgotten that Don had thwarted him and he was supposed to be on his dignity. Always a keen reader of shockers in his spare time, what Don was telling him was meat and drink to him. When Don described his telephone conversation with the man at the Chatham Hotel, Cherry could scarcely contain his excitement.

"Well, that's the story," Don concluded. "I want your help, Cherry. Do you want to get mixed up in this business? I warn you, you may run into trouble. These people appear to stick at nothing. What's it to be?"

"You bet I want..." Cherry began, checked himself hastily as he remembered his position and dignity, coughed, and went on, "Certainly, sir, anything I can do I shall only be too pleased."

Don grinned at him.

"I thought you'd say that. That's fine. You're going to Paris right away. You'll go to the Chatham Hotel and ask for Tregarth. I'm pretty sure he will have gone by the time you get there, but just in case he is still there, make sure he is Tregarth. I'm willing to bet my last buck he's an impostor, but I must be sure." He took from his desk drawer the photograph of Tregarth Hilda had given him. "This is a good likeness of Tregarth. Take it and check it against this man who says he is Tregarth. If he isn't Tregarth, don't let on you know he is an impostor. Tell him I have been called back to London on most urgent business and that I suggest he returns with you and comes to Upper Brook Mews where we can talk. I don't think you will have to do this for a moment. I'm sure our man won't be there. If he isn't, show the photograph to the reception clerk and see if he recognizes Tregarth. Here again, I'm sure he won't be able to. Now can you do all that?"

Cherry moistened his lips and his bright blue eyes gleamed with excitement. This was much more interesting than organizing a string of society parties.

"Certainly, sir. I should behave like an inquiry agent, I take it? What is popularly known as a private eye, I believe."

"That's the idea," Don said, concealing a grin. "But watch out, Cherry. These people are dangerous."

"I shall take every precaution," Cherry returned gravely. "My late master, the Duke, presented me as a parting gift with a sword stick. I have acquired a certain amount of skill with it and any assassin will find I am not easily disposed of, that I can assure you."

Don gaped. The idea of fat Cherry defending himself with a sword struck him as so funny he had difficulty in controlling his features.

"In the meantime, sir," Cherry went on, "what do you intend to do? I take it your plan is to mislead these people into thinking you have gone to Paris when in reality you will remain here?"

"That's the idea," Don said, startled that Cherry should take so easily to this situation. "As soon as we're ready, we'll get Guiseppe to run us over to the Lido airport in the motorboat. I'll fix it with Jack Pleydell to have a plane waiting. We'll fly first to Padua and there I'll leave the plane and return to Venice by train. Jack will take you on to Paris. I'm hoping I've convinced la signorina Natzka that I am going to Paris, but there may

66

be someone at the Paris airport to see if I do arrive. I will tell Jack to go on to London as soon as you have left the plane. I want Jack to pick up Harry and bring him back to Venice. I have an idea I might need him."

Cherry looked relieved.

"I was going to suggest you should send for him, sir. Mason may be a little unruly and there are times when he is an extremely dangerous driver, but he is to be relied on. I'm glad you are having him with you."

"That's settled then. Keep in touch with me through Guiseppe. You know where he lives and he will know at all times where I am." He looked at his watch. "He should be waiting for me now. I said I would see Louisa Peccati's father this afternoon, but that'll have to wait. Go and pack, Cherry, while I fix the plane."

"Yes, sir."

Moving with surprising speed for a man of his age and bulk, Cherry left the room.


A tall, bearded man, wearing a dark blue corduroy suit and a black slouch hat walked down to the embankment from the railway station. He waited with a crowd of newly-arrived tourists while the *vaporetto* edged towards the landing stage.

Hitching up his rucksack, he moved forward as the barrier was let down and took his place against the outer rail with a small group of young Americans who were seeing Venice for the first time.

Not even Don's closest friends would have recognized him now. Arriving at Padua he had gone to a theatrical shop he had dealt with when he had once staged a costume ball at his *palazzo* and there, swearing Benvenuto, the owner of the shop, to secrecy, he had put himself in Benvenuto's hands to alter his appearance. Benvenuto had turned him into a hard-up American artist on a walking tour, and he had excelled himself.

The beard was necessary to hide the Z-shaped scar on Don's cheek, and it bothered him, but he knew he had to put up with it. The clothes, the hat and the heavy walking shoes made him look bigger and heavier than he was, and he was confident no one would recognize him.

He left the boat at the San Zaccaria landing-stage, and walking slowly, he made his way across the *Piazzetta*, past the San Marco basilica and through the shopping quarter towards Guiseppe's modest lodging close to San Maria Formosa.

As he turned the corner of the *calle* he had to make a sharp effort not to check his stride. Just ahead of him, walking slowly, was the man in the white hat.

There was no mistaking the tall, lean figure. He walked leisurely, his hands in his pockets, his white hat at the back of his head, the sun glinting on his gold ear-rings.

Don slightly slowed his pace, wondering if this man's presence so close to Guiseppe's lodgings meant anything.

The man in the white hat glanced over his shoulder. He looked directly at Don who stared at him indifferently, then he looked away and Don breathed again.

At the end of the *calle* was a wine shop, and the man in the white hat went in and sat at a table near the door. Don paused outside the shop, hesitated as any tourist might hesitate, and then entered.

The man in the white hat glanced at him, then glanced away.

Don sat down.

A girl came over to him.

"Vino rose," Don said loudly. "You understand?"

The girl looked at him indifferently, nodded and went over to the man in the white hat who ordered a bottle of white chianti.

Don lit a cigarette and stared through the open door.

The girl brought him a carafe of very indifferent red wine and a glass. She charged him twice as much as the wine was worth, and then she went over to the man in the white hat and served him with the chianti.

"Have you seen il signor Busso this morning?" the man in the white hat asked. "I'm expecting him."

"No, Signor Curizo, I haven't seen him this morning."

The man in the white hat grunted and lighting a cigarette, stretched out his long legs and stared gloomily down at the soiled table top.

Don drank some of his wine, then opening his rucksack, he took out a copy of the Continental *Daily Mail* and glanced at it.

The man in the white hat whom the girl had called Signor Curizo had drunk half his wine before a shadow suddenly darkened the doorway and the short, thick-set man came in.

"I know I'm late," he said, sitting down at Curizo's table, "but my head is very bad. I shouldn't be here."

"Forget your damned head," Curizo snarled. "It was your own fault. I've been waiting twenty minutes for you."

The thick-set man whose name Don guessed was Busso, showed his teeth in a vicious snarl.

"The next time . . ."

"Yes; it is always the next time. There won't be a next time. He's gone to Paris."

"But he will be back."

"By then we won't be here." Curizo got up. "Come on; there are things to do."

Busso grunted as he got to his feet.

"Don't I have time for a drink?"

"No. We're late already. Come on."

They left the wine shop and Don watched them walk down the *calle* and out of sight. He got up quickly and went after them.

He caught sight of them as he turned the corner of the *calle*. They were crossing a *campo*, and as Don watched them, keeping just out of sight, he saw Curizo pause outside a tall, flat-fronted house, take a key from his pocket and open the shabby, black-painted front door.

Both men entered and shut the door behind them.

Don made a mental note of the number of the house and the name of the *campo*, then feeling it would be unwise to venture into the *campo* in case he was seen from one of the windows of the house, he retraced his steps, passed the wine shop and in a few moments was rapping on the door of Guiseppe's lodgings.

Guiseppe himself opened the door.

"Good evening," Don said gruffly. "I understand a gondolier lives here who claims to be the best oarsman in Venice. Is that so?"

Guiseppe drew himself up to his full height and his fierce black eyes flashed.

"I am the best oarsman in Venice," he said loudly. "Who are you and what do you want?"

Don grinned at him.

"Don't you know me, Joe?"

Guiseppe stared, blinked, stared again, then stood aside.

"I did not know you, signore. It is a very fine disguise."

Don entered a large room, sparsely furnished, but clean and orderly.

"I'm without a home at the moment," he said. "Can I make this room my headquarters? I shall only be here a few hours for some sleep, and it won't be for more than a couple of days."

"Certainly, signore," Guiseppe said, his face lighting up. "Consider everything here for what it is as your own."

"Thanks, Joe," Don said. "Now listen, those two fellows we ran into last night have just gone to 22a, Campo de Salizo.

They may live there; they may not. I want the house watched, day and night. Do you know anyone we can trust to do this? I shall want a report on who goes in and comes out. There is a café almost opposite. It shouldn't be difficult."

"That can be arranged," Guiseppe said. "I know the girl who works at the café. She will watch the house until midnight then I will take over. There will be perhaps a little money for her?"

"Pay her what you think," Don said, taking out a roll of Italian currency. He gave Guiseppe a ten thousand lira note. "This should take care of the use of this room and what you pay her. Okay?"

Guiseppe's dark face beamed.

"Yes, signore."

"These two men have seen us together. They mustn't see us together again," Don went on. "I have no immediate job for you, but there will be one before long. Go to this café right away and warn the girl to watch the house. I am going to talk to il signor Peccati. I'll see you back here in about two hours or so."

"I shall be here, signore."

The two men left the room. Guiseppe hurried away to the Campo del Salizo, while Don made his way towards the Fondamente Nuove.

Stefano Peccati sat in a wheeled chair in a small, gloomy room that boasted only of two chairs, a table and a shabby rug.

Peccati's yellow, wrinkled face was set in a cold, stony agony of grief. His legless torso was upright, and he regarded Don with bright, hard, unblinking eyes.

"I cannot see you to-day, signore," he said. "I have just lost my daughter. An old man is entitled to share his sorrow with no one."

"Yes," Don said gently, "but I know something about the way your daughter died. I feel you should know about it."

The old man's face tightened.

"Who are you? What do you know about my daughter?"

"I am Don Micklem. Perhaps your daughter has mentioned my name?"

"I have seen il signore. You are nothing like him. Please go away."

"You have noticed the Z-shaped scar on the right side of Micklem's face?" Don said. "Look, see for yourself," and he carefully parted the false hair that Benvenuto had gummed to

70

his face and leaned forward. "Do you see it?"

Peccati stared at him suspiciously.

"I don't understand."

"Perhaps you will if you will listen to me," Don said. "Does the name John Tregarth mean anything to you?"

By the change of expression in the old man's eyes, Don's question was answered.

"The name is familiar," Peccati said quietly. "What of it?"

"He is a friend of mine and he has disappeared," Don said. "I am looking for him. Two men named Curizo and Busso have some connection with his disappearance. I was told by Tregarth's wife to contact Manrico Rossi who is a business associate of Tregarth. I went to his shop. Your daughter recognized me. She made from a piece of glass Tregarth's initials. It was done in such a way that only I saw it. This action told me she didn't want me to speak to her then. I saw her later. She gave an address to go to after I had told her I was looking for Tregarth. Before she could tell me anything further, Busso surprised and knocked me out. When I recovered, I went immediately to 39, calle Mondello, the address she gave me. It was obviously Tregarth's hiding-place, but he wasn't there. I found your daughter: she had been tortured and murdered."

The old man closed his fists and lowered his head.

Don lit a cigarette and walked over to the window to give the old man time to recover. He turned only when, after a few moments, Peccati said, "Go on, signore, you have more to tell me?"

"Very little more. Since then, every move I have made has been watched. An effort has been made to get me to leave Venice. I decided if I am to solve this mystery I must have freedom of movement. I left Venice, disguised myself as you see and returned. I want as many facts as I can get. I not only want to avenge your daughter, I want also to find Tregarth. Can you help me?"

"How can I help you? I am a helpless cripple," Peccati said bitterly. "If I could, I would. It is not possible."

Don sat down.

"You can help me perhaps by giving me some information. Did you know your daughter and Tregarth knew each other?"

The old man nodded.

"Il signor Tregarth is a very good friend of ours," he said. "He saved the life of my son during the war. My son was an active leader of the resistance movement in Milan. If il signore

71

hadn't supplied arms and money the movement would have failed."

"Where is your son now?" Don asked.

The old man lifted his shoulders.

"I don't know. I haven't heard or seen him for six years The last I heard of him he was in Rome."

"Is Tregarth in Venice now?" Don asked.

"I think he must be," the old man returned. "He may have got away, but I think it is unlikely."

"Will you tell me what happened? Did he come to see you?"

"Yes, he came."

"When was this?"

"Seven days ago. We had gone to bed. About two o'clock in the morning I woke to hear someone knocking on the door. Louisa came into my room. I told her not to answer the door, but she said it was someone who knew the old signal we used during the war: a sign that help was needed. I didn't like her going to the door. As you see, signore, I am old and helpless. There was nothing I could do to protect her, but she insisted on going. It was il signor Tregarth. He was ill and exhausted. Before he collapsed he managed to tell her someone was after him and that he might have been seen coming here. Louisa locked and bolted the door. She dragged il signore into the back room and made him as comfortable as she could. He had been shot: a bad flesh wound across his ribs. It wasn't a new wound: perhaps a fortnight or three weeks old, but it was infected and very painful. He was feverish too. While she dressed the wound, I sat by the windows of the front room in the darkness and watched. I saw two men: a tall man and a short man come along the Fondamente. They passed the house, then after a little while, they returned and went the other way."

"One of these men wore a white hat?" Don asked.

The old man nodded.

"Those two men murdered your daughter," Don said quietly.

"I guessed it," Peccati said. "They must be punished, signore."

"They will be." Don got up and began to move about the room while he considered the information the old man had given him. "How long did Tregarth stay with you?"

"For one day only. He recovered a little of his strength after Louisa had dressed his wound and had given him a meal. I

72

don't know what he told her; not much, I think. I spent most of the time at the window of the front room, keeping watch. She told me a little of what was said when he had gone. He was in bad trouble. He had been followed all the way from Vienna, and twice attempts had been made on his life. He managed to reach Venice, but by then they were close on his heels. They nearly caught him, but he remembered Louisa lived close by and he got under cover just in time."

"Did he say who these people were who are hunting him?"

The old man shook his head.

"We didn't ask. We have learned that no mouth is to be relied on not to talk under pressure. Some talk under little pressure; some talk under great pressure, but sooner or later, they all talk."

"There are exceptions," Don said quietly. "He remained with you for the whole of the next day? Then what happened?"

"He was able to remain with us all that day because it was Sunday, and Louisa didn't have to go to work. Il signor Tregarth said it was necessary for him to find another hiding place. He refused to risk our lives although we both wanted him to stay. He insisted. Louisa knew of this house in the calle della Mondello. No one ever went there. One of the rooms had a bed in it, left by the previous occupier. That night she and il signore went there. It took them a long time as il signore was very weak. He said he would remain there until he got better, then he would try once more to get to England."

"That was what he wanted to do? Return to England?"

"He said it was imperative he should return to England without delay."

If this were true, Don thought, it made nonsense of Sir Robert Graham's theory that Tregarth had gone over to the other side. But how could he be certain it was the truth?

"What happened then? Did he get better?"

"No, signore, he did not get better. The house was damp. Louisa couldn't get to see him to dress his wound as often as was necessary. Il signor Tregarth's fever increased. Two days after he had left here, this man in the white hat came to see Rossi at the shop. Louisa recognized him from my description. Rossi knew Tregarth had once helped our family. This man Curizo – is that his name? – knew Tregarth had vanished near our house. It was simple then for him to suspect we knew where Tregarth was. From then on our house was watched, and Louisa had very great difficulty in seeing il signor Tregarth at all. She warned him that she was being watched. It was then he remembered you were coming to Venice. He had seen it in the newspaper. He wrote a postcard to his London business manager. He was afraid to write direct to his wife in case Louisa was caught posting the card and Curizo saw it. Did you receive the message, signore?"

"Yes. His wife brought it to me."

"This took time. There was now no hope of moving il signor Tregarth; he was too ill. All we could do was to wait for you to come. One night, Curizo came to our house when Louisa was out. He searched it from top to bottom. There was nothing I could do, you understand? I was alone. When he couldn't find il signor Tregarth, he left. He never said one word to me all the time he was in the house. I knew then the situation was now very dangerous for Louisa. I begged her not to go near il signor Tregarth, but she said she couldn't desert him. She went to work the next morning, and that was the last time I saw her. Late last night, the police came to tell me she was dead."

"Do you think Tregarth has escaped?" Don asked.

"I don't know. I think it is very unlikely."

"And you have no idea why these people are so anxious to find him?"

"No, signore, I have no idea."

"I must continue to look for him," Don said. "I will keep in touch with you. You have no one now to care for you?"

The old man shook his head.

"No one, signore."

"Don't worry. I'll fix something for you immediately. Your daughter helped my friend; you won't refuse my help, will you?"

The old man shrugged.

"No, I must accept it, signore. I don't wish it, but I have no choice."

"I'll get someone to come here and look after you," Don said. "You must allow me to see you want for nothing."

"It will not be for long," Peccati returned. "I am old and very tired. Life meant something to me when Louisa was here. It means nothing to me now." He offered his hand. "Thank you for coming, signore. If you wish to make me happy, find and punish those two men."

"I promise you I'll do that," Don said, his face hardening. "I will see you again soon."

It was growing dark as he left the house. Cautiously he paused to look to right and left, before he moved out of the shelter of the dark doorway. Then satisfied there was no one in sight, he slipped down the dark *calle* that ran by the side of the house.

# CHAPTER SEVEN

*Rough House*

---

AN hour later, Don was pacing impatiently up and down Guiseppe's room. From time to time he looked at his watch, lit another cigarette and then continued his pacing.

He was getting worried. Guiseppe should have been back half an hour ago. Had he run into trouble? Don again glanced at his watch. He would give him another five minutes, then he would go and look for him.

Three minutes crawled by, then Don heard the street door open, and a moment later, Guiseppe entered. He was breathing heavily as if he had been running. He spread out his huge hands apologetically as he kicked the door shut.

"I am sorry to have kept you waiting, signore," he said, "but Anita had much to tell me and it is impossible to hurry her."

"I was beginning to worry about you," Don said. "Well, what's the news?"

"I have made some notes so I would remember," Guiseppe said, taking a piece of paper from his hip pocket. "You understand, signore, I am not used to . . ."

"I understand," Don broke in impatiently. "What did she tell you?"

Guiseppe examined the paper with irritating slowness, cleared his throat and spat into the empty fireplace.

"Well, signore, first she saw Manrico Rossi go to the house. He rapped on the door; someone opened it and he entered. Anita knows many people in Venice. She has lived here all her life, and she takes an interest in people. She knew it was Rossi because she has been many times to his shop."

"Okay; so Rossi was the first visitor. Who else?" Don asked, trying to hurry Guiseppe on.

"Then two men she had never seen before came and stood outside the house. They didn't seem too certain that it was the Campo del Salizo. Both these men, she is sure, were German. They were big and strong and not good men. They knocked on the door of the house and went in."

"She was quite sure she hadn't seen them before?"

"Yes, signore. One of them carried a suitcase. She thinks they had only just arrived from the railway station. She doesn't know for certain, you understand, but that is what she thinks."

"Then what happened?"

"An hour passed without anything happening," Guiseppe said, frowning down at his notes. "Then Rossi came out. This will interest you, signore. When he went in, he was swaggering and proud: you understand? When he came out, he was a different man. He looked ill: he was very white, and he walked like an old man. He looked as if he had had a very bad shock: a fright."

"It was dark by then," Don said sharply. "How could she tell?"

"He came to the café and drank three brandies as fast as she could pour them. She asked him if he was ill, but he didn't seem to hear her. He just drank the brandies, paid for them and went out. When he pulled out his money, his hand was shaking so badly, he dropped most of it on the floor."

Don rubbed the back of his neck and stared at Guiseppe.

"He didn't say anything?"

"Nothing at all, signore. He went away, walking slowly like an old man. Then two other men arrived at the house. They paused near the café and Anita had a good view of them. One of them was a tall, thin young man, very blond and handsome. He was well-dressed and rich-looking." Guiseppe scowled. "He made a big impression on Anita who you will understand is only a working girl and whose head is easily turned by riches."

Carl Natzka! Don thought. It must have been he.

"And the other man?" he asked.

"The other man Anita knows well. He was Dr. Avancini; a very fine doctor who has a big practice among the rich people."

"Did they go into the house?"

"Yes, signore, and Anita noticed the doctor carried his bag as if he were going to see a patient."

Don nodded and his eyes brightened. This must mean that Tregarth was in the house! Why else should a doctor be taken there?

"Then what happened?"

"Then I came, signore, and Anita told me, and when I could stop her talking, I ran back here."

"The doctor is still in the house?"

"He was when I left, signore. He may have gone by now."

A sudden sharp rapping on the street door made both men look at each other.

"See who it is," Don said, lowering his voice, "but watch out as you open the door."

Guiseppe went softly into the passage while Don took up his position behind the door where he could see into the passage through the crack between the door and the wall.

"Who is it?" Guiseppe demanded roughly as he half opened the door.

"Blimey! Another Eye-tie," a cheerful cockney voice said. "Can't you speak English, chum?"

Don came out from behind the door and stepped into the passage.

"It's all right, Joe. Let him in."

Suspiciously, Guiseppe stood aside and opened the door.

"Come on in, Harry," Don said. "You've arrived just at the right time."

Harry Mason, Don's chauffeur, walked into the passage. He stopped abruptly, stared at Don, then at Guiseppe, and his sun-tanned face suddenly hardened.

"What's the game?" he demanded. "I thought I heard Mr. Micklem's voice . . ."

"So you did," Don said, smiling. "Don't you recognize me, you dope?"

Harry gaped at him, gulped, took a step forward and peered at him.

"Cor blimey! Is that you, boss? Don't tell me you raised all that fungus since you've been here?"

"Come in and don't talk so much," Don said. "I'm damned glad to see you, Harry. We have a job on, and there's no time for explanations."

He led the way back to Guiseppe's room.

Slightly bewildered, Harry followed him, dumped his suitcase in a corner and looked at Don inquiringly.

"What's up, boss?"

Stocky, broad-shouldered and pugnacious, Harry resembled an aggressive bull mastiff. He was an excellent man to have in any emergency, as Don well knew. During the war he had been a commando, and the hard, tough training had left him with a highly-developed talent for rough-housing and a cold, unshakable nerve.

"A friend of mine is in serious trouble, Harry," Don said. "At the moment he is in the hands of a bunch of thugs, and I have just found out where they are hiding him. We're going to get him out. These fellows stick at nothing. They have already murdered a girl who was helping him. That's how tough they are. I haven't time now to give you details: I'll tell you later. Right now, we've got to get a move on, if we are to get him out."

Harry's face brightened. When he had received Don's telegram to be at the airport, he had guessed Don had stirred up something, but this sounded even better than he had hoped.

"I'm ready when you are, boss," he said.

Don turned to Guiseppe.

"Can we get to the back of the house?"

"It is backed by a *rio*, signore. We could go in my gondola."

"We can't hope to surprise them if we go in the front way. We'd better take a look at the back of the house. But, first, find out if anything has happened at the house since you were there. Meet us at the gondola station, and be as quick as you can."

"Yes, signore," Guiseppe said and went quickly from the room.

"Come on," Don said to Harry. "We'll get down to the gondola."

As they hurried through the dark *calli* Don gave Harry a very brief sketch of what had been happening since he had arrived in Venice.

"From what Peccati tells me," Don said as they reached the gondola station, "Tregarth is pretty ill. We have a job on our hands, but the three of us should be able to handle it. When we get him out, we'll take him to my place. Then we must decide what to do with him."

"These blokes won't like parting with him, will they, boss?" Harry said with a grin.

"They won't, but I daresay we'll persuade them to change their minds."

At this moment Guiseppe came running along the *molo*.

"No one has left the house yet, signore," he panted as he came up.

"The doctor's still there?"

"Yes, signore. No one has left."

"Okay. Let's take a look at the back of the house. There are too many in there for us at the moment, but at least we can look. Come on; let's go."

The long, black gondola slid through the darkness of the narrow *rio*, its lantern shedding a faint yellow light on the still waters. The big moon lit up the roof tops of the buildings on either side of the *rio*, but failed to penetrate below the top floor windows.

It was so dark Don wondered how Guiseppe knew where he was going, and Harry, who had never been in a gondola, stared uneasily out of the cabin window, expecting the boat to crash at any moment into some unseen obstacle.

Guiseppe said suddenly, "We're close now, signore. Shall I put out the light?"

"I'll do it," Don said, and leaving the cabin, he moved forward and doused the flickering flame.

A few more strokes of the oar brought them close to the black outline of a house.

Harry crawled out of the cabin and joined Don. They both stared up at the dark house towering above them. No lights showed. Ten feet above their heads they could see the outline of a balcony. Another ten feet higher up the moonlight lit up a small, iron-barred window.

As far as they could see the wall of the house was as smooth as glass with no foot or hand holds to assist a climb.

"If we had a rope and a hook, boss," Harry muttered, "I could get up there as easy as kiss your hand."

Don nodded.

"That's what we want. I can't see if the window's barred like the one above, can you?"

Harry shook his head.

"It could be, boss. If this bloke's ill, we'll have a job getting him down, bars or no bars. We want a stretcher to make a job of it."

Don thought so too.

"Our best way is to go in at the back and come out by the front." He turned to Guiseppe. "We want a rope and a strong hook, Joe."

"They'll have rope at the café, signore. We had better go back," Guiseppe said.

He turned the gondola, and after a few minutes of swift rowing, he brought the gondola to the side of the *molo*.

"If you wait here, signore, I'll get what you want."

"We'll come with you." Don touched Harry's arm. "I want you to take a look at the front of the house."

The three of them cut down a *calle* that brought them into the Campo del Salizo.

While Guiseppe crossed the *campo* and went into the café,

Don and Harry remained out of sight in the dark mouth of the *calle*.

"That's the house," Don said, pointing.

As he spoke the front door opened and Carl Natzka came out. He paused at the top of the steps to light a cigarette. He was followed by a fat, elderly man who Don guessed was Dr. Avancini. Together they walked down the steps, crossed the *campo* and disappeared into the darkness.

"If that girl knows how to count," Don went on, "that leaves four men in there. I guess we can tackle four if we surprise them."

Harry nodded.

Guiseppe came from the café, carrying a coil of thin rope and a heavy hook. He joined Don and Harry in the mouth of the *calle*.

"Fine," Don said, examining the rope. "That's the very thing." He went on to Harry, "You go with Joe and get in at the back. I'll give you ten minutes, then I'll go in the front. Don't start anything until I arrive, unless you have to."

"Suppose the window's barred, boss?" Harry said. "I don't want you to walk in there alone."

"If it's barred, come around to the front as fast as you can. Okay?"

Harry nodded. He never wasted words when action was pending.

"Take him to the back of the house," Don said to Guiseppe. "As soon as he's up on the balcony and if he can get in, tie up your boat and come around to the front of the house. You'll find me in there."

"Yes, signore," Guiseppe said, and he flexed his great muscles as if he were already anticipating a battle.

He and Harry went back to the gondola while Don leaned against the wall and waited.

The minutes crawled by. Don kept peering at his watch while he wondered if Harry would be able to get into the house. He wondered, too, if Tregarth were really there, and he realized, if he had any luck, this could be the final move in the hunt.

It seemed to him an hour had crawled by before the hands of his watch told him it was time to take action. Moving out of the dark *calle*, he crossed the *campo*, walked briskly up the steps of the house and rapped sharply on the black-painted front door.

There was a long pause, then as he lifted his hand to rap again,

81

he heard someone coming. The front door jerked open and Busso, short, thick-set and menacing, stood in the doorway and glared up at him.

"What do you want?" he asked roughly.

"I have an urgent call for Doctor Avancini," Don said, edging forward. "I was told he is here."

"Well, he isn't ..." Busso began, then the rest of his sentence was choked off by a grunt of anguish as Don's fist slammed into his stomach.

Busso doubled up, gasping, and Don's fist flashed up and smashed against the side of his jaw.

"Just a little of your own medicine, fatso," Don said softly, grabbing hold of Busso as his knees buckled. He lowered him gently to the floor, stepped over him into a dimly-lit passage and closed the front door.

Well, at least he was inside the house, Don thought as he blew on his smarting knuckles while his eyes took in the lay-out of the ground floor.

A steep flight of stairs faced him. There was a door to his right and another door at the far end of the passage.

He stood listening for a moment. A murmur of men's voices came from the door at the far end of the passage, but he could hear no other sounds.

He decided to go up the stairs in the hope of joining forces with Harry. But as he moved forward, he heard the sound of a door opening on the upper landing, and he quickly ducked back into the shadow of the staircase.

Footfalls thudded across the landing.

"Busso? Who was it?"

Peering through the banister rail, Don caught a glimpse of Curizo as he stood at the head of the stairs.

Don waited, his muscles tense.

Curizo began to descend the stairs. Halfway down he caught sight of Busso lying in the shadows. He stopped abruptly, leaned forward and peered at Busso.

Don heard him curse softly, then Curizo came down the rest of the stairs with a rush. He bent over Busso, but not long enough for Don to reach him. He turned with the quickness of a striking snake as Don slid out of his hiding-place.

For a split second the two men looked at each other, then Curizo's hand flashed behind him and Don jumped forward.

He anticipated Curizo's body swerve to the left, and his questing hand grabbed Curizo by the throat while his left hand slammed a punch to Curizo's jaw.

But Curizo wasn't so easily caught. He threw up his arm and just managed to block the punch, and countered with a raking left that drove Don back a step.

As Don's fingers slid off Curizo's throat, he grabbed him by his coat front, leaned back and jerked hard.

Curizo lost his balance. Stepping to one side, Don kicked Curizo's ankle and brought him heavily to the floor.

"Hans!" Curizo yelled as he drove his foot into Don's chest, sending him staggering back. "Hans!"

The door at the end of the passage jerked open and a big, swarthy man who Don guessed would be Hans sprang into the passage. He was followed by a big, blond man who tried to shove Hans out of his way to get at Don.

The two men hampered each other in the narrow passage, giving Don a chance to gain the stairs. He had one foot on the third stair when Curizo, still on the floor, heaved himself forward and grabbed at Don's ankle, bringing him face down on the stairs.

Don kicked back savagely and the heel of his shoe caught Curizo's shoulder, flinging him back.

By now Hans had reached the foot of the stairs. He jumped over Curizo, his brutal heavy face vicious. He reached out to grab Don who ducked under the questing hands, straightened up and slammed home a punch to Hans' heart that brought him down on hands and knees.

Don turned and scrambled up three more stairs before the blond man who was crouching against the other side of the banisters suddenly straightened, reached over the banisters and caught Don's wrist and yanked him against the banisters.

The blond man's grip was paralysing and Don couldn't break free.

Hans got off his knees and looked up at Don, his lips off his teeth. He came up the stairs swinging a fist the size of a melon and aimed a blow that would have taken Don's head off if it had landed, but Don just managed to duck in time.

Cursing, Hans started another crushing punch, but before the blow could land, Harry appeared on the upper landing, saw what was happening and launched himself down the stairs, feet first.

His feet crashed into Hans, swept him down the stairs with

Harry on top of him. They landed in the passage with a crash that shook the house.

Don put his free hand on the banister rail and vaulted over it, landing on top of the blond man and they went down in a heap. The blond man's great hands fastened on Don's throat and nipped his breath off.

Don rammed his thumbs into the blond man's eyes. The agonizing grip on his throat fell away and the blond man snatched at Don's wrists, yelling with pain.

Harry had tossed Hans over his head and Hans crashed against the door at the end of the passage. As Harry turned to go after him, Curizo closed with him.

To get to close quarters with Harry was like getting to close quarters with a buzz-saw. A shower of half-arm punches slammed into Curizo's stomach and under his heart, punches that felt like the blows of a sledge hammer. Curizo's knees buckled, he tried to break away, then he saw a fist flash up and he took a punch on the jaw that flattened him.

Don was still struggling with the blond man.

Harry gave the two men a quick glance, saw Don was more than holding his own, jumped over their struggling bodies to close with Hans who was now staggering to his feet.

Then Busso suddenly came to life. He got up on hands and knees. He saw Don kneeling on top of the blond man, choking the life out of him. He saw Harry, his head buried on Hans' chest, his arms working like pistons, and the look of agony on Hans' face as his ribs bent under the crushing blows.

Busso pulled a knife, got to his feet and crept towards Don.

At this moment the front door burst open and Guiseppe stormed in.

Busso spun around, slashed at Guiseppe as Guiseppe bounded towards him.

Guiseppe dodged and closing his great fist he slammed it down on top of Busso's head. Busso dropped like a pole-axed bull.

Don had finished off the blond man and he staggered to his feet. He looked quickly to see how Harry was getting on.

Harry was enjoying himself. He was kneeling on Hans while he methodically choked the breath out of him. There was a sudden flurry of kicking, a gasping rattle and Hans went limp.

Harry sat back on his heels and surveyed the limp body with professional interest.

"He'll be quiet for the next twenty minutes," he said and got to his feet.

Don leaned against the wall, breathing heavily. He looked around the battlefield with satisfaction.

"Pretty nice work," he panted.

The blond man, Busso and Curizo lay in limp attitudes on the floor.

"You all right, boss?" Harry asked, unmindful of a trickle of blood that ran down his own face and an eye that was beginning to puff.

"I'm fine," Don said. "Phew! I guess I must be a little out of training. That was quite warm while it lasted. We'd better tie these guys up before they start trouble again. While you two are taking care of them, I'll look around."

He stepped over Hans' body and looked into the room at the end of the passage. There was no one in it. Turning, he picked his way over the other bodies to look into the room on the right of the front door. That room, too, was empty.

If Tregarth were anywhere, he'd be upstairs, Don told himself, and went up the stairs three at the time.

The two rooms on the next floor were also empty, and he went on up the next flight of stairs.

Facing him was a door which was bolted on the outside and he paused outside it.

As he pulled back the bolt on the outside, he became aware that his heart was beating rapidly. With any luck Tregarth was in this room, and he had succeeded in less time than he had thought possible in finding him.

He pushed open the door.

The room was small. Two candles, stuck in bottles, their flames flickering, made a shadowy light. The only article of furniture in the room was a camp bed, and on the bed lay a man, naked to the waist.

He lay in the semi-darkness and he didn't move as Don crossed quickly to the mantelpiece and picked up one of the candles.

Don held the light above his head and stepped to the bed.

Although he hadn't seen John Tregarth for so many years, he immediately recognized him. Although he was emaciated and the sides of his dark hair were now grey, there was no mistaking the firm, determined face.

He lay motionless, his eyes closed, and his face was so white that for a moment Don thought he was dead. Then he saw a

85

slight movement of his chest as he breathed, and he saw something else, too: something that made him feel a little sick and
turned him cold.

All over Tregarth's naked chest were small brown burns: the
same kind of burns Don had seen covering Louisa Peccati's right
hand: cigarette burns. On the left side of Tregarth's chest was
a dirty, bloodstained pad strapped to his emaciated ribs by two
broad strips of adhesive tape.

Don bent forward and gently touched Tregarth's arm.

"John! Can you hear me?"

Tregarth didn't move nor did he give any sign that he had
heard. The slight, irregular lift of his chest as he breathed was
the only sign that he was alive.

Harry came into the room.

"Have you found him, boss?"

"Yes, he's here," Don said. "He's bad. The swine have been
torturing him."

Harry joined him at the bed. He sucked in his breath sharply
when he saw the burns.

"He looks pretty far gone," Don went on, "but we've got to
get him out of here."

Harry took Tregarth's wrist in his fingers and felt his pulse.

"Yes, he's bad all right. He could die on us."

Don went to the door and called down to Guiseppe to come
up.

"We'll wrap him in the blanket and Guiseppe can carry him,"
he said to Harry. "We'll get him to the gondola."

Guiseppe entered the room.

"We want to get him to the boat, Joe," Don said, waving to
Tregarth. "You can carry him, can't you?"

Guiseppe stared down at Tregarth.

"Yes, signore. There's no weight there. Is he alive?"

"Just about."

Harry was wrapping the blanket around Tregarth, then he
stood aside while Guiseppe bent and scooped Tregarth gently
off the bed, holding him in his arms.

"Can you manage?" Don asked.

"It is nothing, signore."

"Let's get out of here," Don said and led the way out of the
room and down the stairs.

The four men, now securely trussed with rope, were still
unconscious, and, after a quick look at them, Don stepped to
the front door, opened it and looked out on to the deserted

*campo*. The only light that showed came from the café opposite.

"All clear at the moment," he said, and went down the steps, followed by Guiseppe carrying Tregarth and by Harry who shut the front door after him.

The three of them crossed the *campo* and went down the dark *calle* that led to the *molo* where the gondola had been left.

Harry paused to look back. His keen eyes searched the dark doorway and the mouths of two dark *calli* on the far side of the *campo*.

Out of one of the *calli* came two men. They saw Harry at the same time as he saw them.

One of them turned swiftly and disappeared. The other came to an abrupt standstill.

"Let's move, boss," Harry said, catching up with Don. "Looks like we've got company."

# CHAPTER EIGHT

*The Shrine*

---

OUT of the silence and the darkness of the night, there came a loud, shrill whistle.

"As fast as you can, Joe," Don said, falling back. "Get him to the boat."

He turned to join Harry who was standing in a doorway, looking back down the dark *calle*.

"There were two of them, boss," Harry said softly. "But it sounds as if there're more coming now."

Don listened to the sound of footfalls, and nodded.

"Some of them are going down the next *calle*. They'll head Joe off if he isn't quick. We'd better go with him, Harry. Come on."

He broke into a run, and followed by Harry, he pelted down the *calle*, catching up with Guiseppe as he trotted into the darkness. He slid past him and went on in front while Harry kept just behind Guiseppe.

Harry could hear the soft pad-pad of footfalls in his rear. Whoever was following him made no effort to overtake him, and Harry guessed he was there merely to block a retreat.

Don was the first to see the three men lurking in the shadows by the boat. He had reached the mouth of the *calle* and he pulled up short, stopping Guiseppe.

"Wait!" he whispered and peered cautiously around the corner, looking at the three men who hadn't yet seen him, although they were staring in his direction. "Harry and I will take them on. Your job is to get il signore to your boat. Don't wait for us. Take him to your place."

Guiseppe, breathing hard, nodded.

Harry slid up.

"There's a bloke behind us, boss," he warned.

"Three of them are guarding the gondola," Don said. "Joe's going on ahead. We'll handle these three."

"When you're ready, boss."

"Let's go."

Both of them shot out of the dark mouth of the *calle* as if they had been propelled by a gun.

The three men saw them coming. They wavered before the

determined rush, opened out, each trying to avoid the first clash.

Knives gleamed in the darkness as Don, reaching the first man, swerved from a knife thrust, bent, caught the man's ankle and heaved. The man went over backwards and landed on his head, stiffened and stretched out.

Harry was at grips with the second man. The force of his rush brought them both to the cobblestones. They grappled for each other's throats.

For a few furious moments the four men struggled, punched and cursed each other. Then as Don was getting the upper hand of his man, a fourth man appeared and dropped on Don's back. Fingers like steel closed around Don's throat. The man he was kneeling on got one hand free and smashed his fist into Don's face, stunning him.

Don tried to break the hold on his throat, but he was too stunned to do more than grope at the hooked fingers that sank into his flesh. Blood began to pound in his head, and he felt himself blacking out. He got another punch in the face, and desperately he heaved himself up and threw himself sideways. He rolled off the *molo* into the cold waters of the *rio*.

He took with him the man who was choking him. The steel fingers left his throat and he heaved himself upwards, his head breaking clear of the water.

His opponent came to the surface at the same time, spluttering and cursing in Italian.

The shock of the cold water brought Don to his senses. He took in a great gasp of air, then let himself sink. He reached out, his hands caught hold of his opponent's coat and he dragged him down.

One of Don's pet sports was water-polo, and what he didn't know about underwater tackling wasn't worth knowing. He had his opponent helpless in a head lock, his legs around the other's waist. His fingers shifted to the man's throat, found the main artery and squeezed. With a frantic spasm the man blacked out. Don released him and bobbed to the surface.

"You there, boss?" Harry's voice asked cheerfully out of the darkness.

"Here," Don said, shaking the water out of his eyes. He took two powerful strokes forward and joined Harry who was treading water in the middle of the *rio*.

"Blimey! There were dozens of the perishers," Harry said softly. "It got too hot for me. I dived in when I saw you go in. They're along the bank, waiting for us."

"What about Joe?"

"He's taken the boat and hooked it."

"Come on. Don't make too much noise. I don't think they can see us."

They began to swim silently down the *rio*, keeping in its dark centre, but as soon as they moved they heard the pad-pad of footfalls along the *molo*, keeping pace with them.

"Still got company, boss," Harry whispered.

Don glanced over his shoulder. His sharp ears had heard a faint swishing sound not far off.

"There's a gondola coming," he said. "Watch out, Harry. If they're after us, they may take a smack at your head with the oar as they pass."

"That's nice," Harry muttered. "That's very nice."

"Tread water and face about," Don whispered. "Dive as soon as you see the boat."

A big black gondola, without lights, suddenly appeared out of the darkness. It was moving fast, and it was on them before Don had finished speaking.

Don dropped his legs and went down like a stone. Where his head had been a moment before, he heard a dull, violent splash. He had guessed right: the gondolier had struck at his head with the oar and had only just missed.

Don gave a kick and came to the surface. He caught sight of Harry's head bobbing within a few feet of him, and both men looked for the gondola.

It had stopped. They could just make out the gondolier against the dark background of the houses, furiously reversing the boat.

"Let's have him in," Don muttered. "One each side of him. Don't let him catch you with the oar."

"I'll take his attention, boss. You grab his legs."

The gondola was nearly on them now. Harry bobbed out of the water and waved.

The gondolier lifted and swung his oar. Don took two strokes forward, reached the stern of the boat, heaved himself up and made a grab at the gondolier's legs. He caught at a trouser cuff, hung on and heaved backwards.

The gondolier, off balance as he swung the oar, gave an ear-splitting yell, dropped his oar and belly-flopped into the water.

Harry swam over to him, and, as he came to the surface, Harry shot out his fist, catching the gondolier between the eyes. He went down with a great rush of bubbles, and without waiting to see if he was coming up again, Harry swam over to the floating oar.

The gondola, out of control, swung half round.

Don caught hold of the stern, pulled himself up and got on board. Harry grabbed the floating oar, swam to the side of the gondola, handed up the oar, then pulled himself on board.

"Can you handle her, boss?" he asked, squatting on the floor of the gondola.

"Sure," Don said, fitting the oar into the rowlock. "Joe thinks he's the best oarsman in Venice; watch me."

He straightened the gondola, keeping it in mid-stream, then he began to row. He sent the big black boat shooting into the darkness, and, in a few moments, the sound of running feet on the *molo* faded away, as the gondola sped out into the open *canale* where it couldn't be followed.

The two bronze giants on top of Coducci's clock tower were striking midnight as Don and Harry moved silently down the dark, deserted *calle* that led to Guiseppe's lodgings.

They had left the gondola moored to the landing-stage of the San Zaccaria *vaporetti* station, and, after taking precautions to make sure they weren't being followed, they went with all speed to rejoin Guiseppe.

Both of them were dripping water, but the night was warm, and neither of them felt cold.

"Here we are," Don said, pausing outside Guiseppe's house. "Will I be glad to get rid of these wet whiskers!"

"They suit you, boss," Harry said, grinning in the darkness. "I wish Miss Rigby could see you now."

Don rapped on the door.

After a moment's delay, Guiseppe asked, "Who is it?" He didn't open the door.

"He's learning fast," Don said to Harry, then raising his voice, he called, "Okay, Joe, let us in."

The door opened, and Guiseppe, his eyes gleaming with excitement, stood aside.

"How is he?" Don asked, crossing the passage and entering Guiseppe's room.

"Just the same, signore. He hasn't moved or opened his eyes. I have been very careful with him."

Don went over to where Tregarth lay on the bed, still wrapped in the blanket. He looked at him, took his pulse, then shook his head.

"You'd better get out of those wet things, boss," Harry said, already stripping off his clothes. "I've got a change here for you." He went over to his suitcase and tossed a shirt, sweater and a pair of flannel trousers in Don's direction. "They'll be a tight fit, but they'll be better than those wet things."

While Don stripped off and rubbed himself dry with a rough towel Guiseppe gave him, Guiseppe brewed up three large mugs of black coffee.

Changed and dry again, Don removed the false beard, grimacing as he stripped the gummed canvas from his face.

"Phew! That's better," he said, rubbing his sore face. "Are you all right, Harry?"

Harry was examining his black eye in the small mirror above the fireplace.

"I'm fine, boss. I've got a nice shiner, but what's a shiner between friends?" He looked over at Tregarth. "What are we going to do with him?"

"Take him home," Don said. "I'll get Pleydell to organize a plane and we'll fly him back."

"We've got to get him to the airfield first," Harry said. "I have an idea those perishers won't let us do exactly what we like."

"We'll take the motor-boat. So long as they don't find us here. I don't see how they can stop us once we're in the motor-boat."

Guiseppe handed round mugs of steaming coffee.

Don drank some of the coffee, lit a cigarette, then went over to Tregarth. He bent over him.

The thin emaciated face was the colour of old ivory; the slack lips were a bluish tinge, the deep sunk eyes were still hidden by dark, heavy eyelids.

"He worries me," Don said. "I think we should get a doctor to look at him." He straightened and turned to Guiseppe. "Do you know a doctor we can trust, Joe?"

Guiseppe nodded.

"Dr. Vergellesi is a good man, signore. He lives not far from here. Shall I get him?"

Don hesitated. He felt Tregarth's pulse, then alarmed at the feeble response, he nodded.

"You'd better, Joe. He's nearly done."

Guiseppe went quickly from the room.

Harry came over and stood looking down at Tregarth.

"He does look bad," he said. "Do you know what it's all about, boss?"

"I haven't an idea," Don said, pulling up a chair and sitting down close to Tregarth. "I've been asking myself what the mess is he's got himself into. What's been happening to him? Why have they been torturing him like this?"

As if in answer to his questions, Tregarth's eyes suddenly opened. He looked fixedly at Don, and Don felt a little chill creep up his spine. The eyes were already dead: glazed and expressionless and lifeless. Tregarth's lips twitched and his head moved.

"John!" Don said sharply. "It's Micklem. Can you hear me? It's Don Micklem."

Very slowly the head turned in his direction. The lifeless eyes stared past his face as he leaned forward.

"John! You're safe!" he said, raising his voice. "It's Micklem. Don't you know me?"

Tregarth shuddered. His eyes suddenly came alive and he stared up at Don.

Don picked up the lamp on the table and held it so Tregarth could see him clearly.

"You're safe, fella," he said. "Just take it easy. Don't try to talk."

"He could do with a drink, boss," Harry said. "A little wine and water won't hurt him."

He went across to where Guiseppe kept a carafe of water and a couple of bottles of wine and quickly mixed the drink and brought it over.

While Don lifted Tregarth's head, Harry gave him the drink.

Tregarth took some of the wine and water. He closed his eyes and Don let him down gently on the pillow again.

Both men looked anxiously at the white, twitching face.

For a long moment Tregarth remained motionless, then he opened his eyes and looked searchingly at Don. He looked from Don to Harry and back to Don again.

"It's all right," Don said, guessing Tregarth was worried by Harry's presence. "He's one of us. He works for me. He and I got you out."

Tregarth's lips moved. He muttered something that Don couldn't hear.

"Don't try to talk," Don said. "Just take it easy."

Again Tregarth's lips moved. Bending low over him, Don just managed to catch the muttered words.

93

"Dei Fabori . . . Shrine . . ."

The effort of speaking was too much for Tregarth. His eyelids dropped and he drifted into unconsciousness.

Don straightened up.

"He was trying to tell me something," he said as Harry looked questioningly at him. "What did he mean? Dei Fabori, and then the word shrine? There's a calle dei Fabori." He suddenly snapped his fingers. "That's right. In the calle dei Fabori there is a wall shrine to the Virgin Mother. Now, what was he driving at?"

They heard the street door open, and both of them stepped quickly to the door, Harry sliding behind it while Don opened it.

Guiseppe, followed by a tall, elderly man in black, had just entered the passage.

"This is Dr. Vergellesi," Guiseppe said.

"I'm Don Micklem." Don shook hands with the doctor. "A friend of mine is seriously ill. He has got into some trouble with a political organization. I don't know the details, but he has been wounded and tortured. This is not a matter for the Italian police, signore. The British Consul will be informed, and I must ask you to say nothing of the matter."

Vergellesi looked sharply at Don, his bushy eyebrows climbing.

"I'm afraid I can't do that. If il signore has been wounded it is my duty to report to the police."

"My friend is a British subject. It is not a matter for the Italian police."

Vergellesi lifted his shoulders.

"If he is British, then that is another matter. Perhaps I had better see him."

Don led the way into Guiseppe's room and stood at the head of the bed while Vergellesi examined Tregarth. It didn't take him a minute or so to come to a conclusion.

Gently he covered Tregarth's mutilated chest and straightened.

"Il signore is dangerously ill," he said. "He must be taken to hospital immediately. He has acute pneumonia and is suffering from exposure and severe shock."

"Can't he be taken to my house, doctor?" Don asked. "You need spare no expense. I don't want him to go to hospital if it can be avoided."

Vergellesi shook his head.

"He must go to hospital immediately. We have the equipment there to save his life. He must be put in an oxygen tent within half an hour or he will die."

"All right." Don turned to Harry. "Go with him and don't leave him for a second, Harry. I'll be along in a couple of hours to relieve you."

"Okay, boss," Harry said.

Vergellesi looked uneasily at Don.

"You speak as if il signore is still in danger. Would it not be better to inform the police?"

"Not until I have spoken to the British Consul," Don said. "How are we to get him to hospital?"

"Could one of you carry him to a gondola?" Vergellesi asked. "I could have a stretcher brought, but time means everything."

Guiseppe said, "I can do it, signore."

"Very well. We will go at once. I will go ahead to arrange a room for him," Vergellesi said.

"Will you save him, doctor?" Don asked anxiously.

"I hope so. It depends a lot on his own stamina. He has a chance, anyway."

"I'll come with you as far as the gondola," Don said to Guiseppe.

Vergellesi moved to the door.

"I will have everything ready for him by the time you get there," he said. "In two hours I will be able to tell if I can save him."

"I'll see you then, doctor," Don said.

Vergellesi hurried from the room.

"You go on ahead, Harry," Don said. "Keep your eyes open." He turned to Guiseppe as Harry went off, "Sure you can manage, Joe?"

"It is nothing, signore," Guiseppe said and gently picked up the unconscious man.

After waiting a moment or so to give Harry a chance to look around, they left the room and walked silently down the *calle* to where Guiseppe had moored his gondola. They met no one, and when they reached the boat, Harry was in it, waiting for them. He helped Guiseppe lower Tregarth into the boat.

"As quick as you can," Don said. "I'll be at the hospital in an hour or so."

"Okay, boss," Harry said. "I'll take care of him."

Don stood on the *molo* and watched the gondola move swiftly down the dark *rio*. He waited until it was out of sight, then he set off with long, quick strides towards the calle dei Fabori.

The calle dei Fabori lay in the centre of the tourist sight-seeing district, and when Don eventually reached it he found he had by no means the long *calle* to himself.

Ahead of him he could see a small group of American tourists; behind them wandered two elderly women with an elderly male escort and behind them, arm-in-arm were an obvious honey-mooning couple.

Don remembered that the little wall shrine was towards the Rialto Bridge end of the *calle*. It wasn't going to be easy to examine, he thought, with so many people about.

Why had Tregarth mentioned the shrine? Had he left a message there or hidden something there? Was the shrine in some way connected with the mystery of his disappearance? Had he known what he was saying or had he been delirious?

Don paused in a dark doorway to let the people ahead of him go on. He glanced back over his shoulder, but the lighted *calle* stretched emptily back towards the rear of San Marco.

Ahead of him he could just see the faint light of the lamp before the wall shrine. The elderly trio passed it without appearing to notice it. The group of Americans paused for a moment to stare at the shrine, then they too went on, but the young couple stopped to admire it.

Don waited impatiently.

"What a lovely idea," the girl said, her young voice coming clearly to Don. "Isn't it a pretty thing, Jack?"

Her escort slid his arm around her and pulled her to him.

"It's all right I suppose but I don't believe in that kind of thing. And talking about pretty things, you should look in a mirror one of these days."

The girl laughed.

"I wonder if you'll be saying that to me in ten years' time."

"The answer to that one is wait and see. Come on, let's find somewhere to eat. I'm starving."

Don was relieved to see them move on.

He walked quickly to the shrine.

It was a small affair: no more than a hole in the wall and protected by iron bars. It contained a little statue of the Virgin Mary, a spray of artificial flowers in a metal vase and a small oil lamp to light the shrine.

He examined the shrine carefully, but could see nothing that could have the remotest connection with Tregarth.

96

Disappointed, he moved away. Then he paused, frowning. There must be something there he hadn't seen. Tregarth had been so determined to tell him about the shrine. He went back and stared again into the lighted crevice.

He decided the only place anything could be concealed in was the metal vase.

With difficulty he squeezed his hand between the iron bars and tilted the vase towards him.

There was something there beside the artificial flowers! He pulled the vase close to the bars, then lifted out the flowers.

Wedged down in the funnel of the vase was a small green oil-skin package.

Don hooked out the package, and as he did so, he instinctively looked down the *calle*.

Coming towards him were two men: one of them had a white hat – it was Curizo!

Don stepped back, the package in his hand.

Curizo broke into a run, followed by the other man whom Don recognized as the brutish Hans.

Don spun on his heel and ran. Pelting down the *calle,* he reached the quay that ran along the Grand Canale and found himself immediately hemmed in by a packed, slowly-moving crowd of sightseers.

He dropped the package into his pocket, and slackening his pace to a crawl, he threaded his way through the crowd, knowing that Curizo and Hans were close on his heels.

He glanced back over his shoulder.

Curizo was within six feet of him. They looked at each other and Don grinned. Curizo's dark eyes were glittering, and his thin mouth snarled.

Knowing neither of the men dared attack him in this vast crowd, Don kept on towards the *Palazzo della Toletta*.

Curizo and Hans followed him, keeping a few yards behind him.

Along the entire length of the *fondamente* the close-packed crowd moved slowly towards the *San Marco piazza*. As Don came into sight of his *palazzo* he suddenly quickened his pace.

He edged sideways into the crowd, apologizing as he forced his way through. Then suddenly free of the crowd, he reached the steps of the *palazzo* and ran up them. He opened the front door and stepped into the hall.

He paused to look back.

Curizo and Hans kept on. Neither of them looked at him, and

Don was a little surprised they had given up so tamely although he realized there was nothing they could do before such a vast audience.

He shut the door, shot the bolts and drew in a quick sigh of relief.

But his feeling of security didn't last a couple of seconds.

He became aware how silent the house was. Mario, the under-footman, who took charge in Cherry's absence, and who should have been in the hall, wasn't to be seen. Then Don noticed there was a light showing under his study door.

He stepped softly across the hall, took the oilskin package from his pocket and put it into a copper bowl that stood on a finely-carved Venetian table.

He had just time to move away from the table when his study door opened and Carl Natzka appeared in the doorway.

"Good evening, Mr. Micklem," he said gently and smiled. "Please forgive this intrusion, but I am very anxious to talk to you."

Don moved across the hall and Natzka stepped aside so Don could enter.

"Nice to see you," Don said. "I hope I haven't kept you waiting," and he walked into the study.

Busso and the blond man were standing against the wall. Busso held a blunt-nosed automatic and as Don came in, he lifted it and pointed it at him.

# CHAPTER NINE

## ...Or Else

CARL NATZKA closed the door and leaned his back against it.

"Forgive me for being so dramatic, Mr. Micklem," he said, "but the past few hours have shown that you are a man of violence. Busso's gun is effectively silenced, and he has orders to shoot you if the need arises. It is extremely important that we should talk without interruption."

"By all means," Don said, and crossing over to his favourite chair he sat down. "By the way, how is your charming sister?"

Natzka smiled.

"A little anxious about you, Mr. Micklem. She is young and susceptible, and she has taken a liking to you as I have. I am embarrassed to have to threaten you in this way, but the situation is critical and I have no alternative. I can assure you the last thing I would wish to do is to harm you."

Don grinned.

"That's fine; I share the sentiment with you." He reached into the cigar box on the table, selected a cigar and raised it, looking at Natzka. "Will you smoke?"

"I think not," Natzka said and came to sit near Don.

Don lit the cigar in an atmosphere that had suddenly become tense. He blew smoke towards the ceiling, crossed one leg over the other and looked at Natzka.

"Well, now, what is it you want to talk to me about?"

"About Tregarth." Natzka laced his fingers together and rested them on his knees. "Tregarth is an Englishman; you are an American. Tregarth has got himself involved in an affair of State. I am hoping that you will be intelligent, Mr. Micklem, and declare yourself neutral. This matter is really between the British government and my government. It has nothing to do with the United States: nothing whatsoever, and I am only asking you not to interfere or obstruct either government."

"That's reasonable," Don returned. "I have no wish to interfere with any government."

Natzka nodded, his slate grey eyes watchful.

"In that case I am sure you will hand over the package in green oilskin that you now have."

Don looked with interest at his cigar, then glanced at Natzka, raising his eyebrows.

"An oilskin package? What makes you think I have an oilskin package?"

Natzka's face tightened and his eyes turned cold.

"Don't let us waste time, Mr. Micklem," he said. "You have just said you were ready to co-operate. This package..."

"One moment," Don said, raising his hand. "I didn't say I would co-operate. I said I wouldn't interfere between governments. That is a vastly different thing to my thinking. Tell me about the package. Does it belong to you?"

"It belongs to my government. It was stolen from our Foreign Office by Tregarth."

"And why should Tregarth steal it?"

"It contains valuable information, Mr. Micklem: valuable to another Power. I have orders to get the package back, and I intend to do so."

"Surely it was very careless of your Foreign Office to allow Tregarth to obtain this information if it is so valuable?" he said mildly.

Natzka nodded.

"Extremely careless, but then Tregarth is an exceedingly clever man. I should like to congratulate you on the way you rescued him by the way. It was very handsomely done."

"It wasn't so bad," Don said and smiled. "But your henchmen aren't particularly good in a rough house."

"That may be," Natzka said, "but they have talents in other directions. They can persuade people to talk, Mr. Micklem."

"Can they? They appear to have failed to make Tregarth talk, otherwise you would scarcely be wasting your time here."

"Tregarth would have talked," Natzka said. "It was merely a matter of time. He was a sick man, Mr. Micklem; Busso had to be careful. If he had been stronger, Busso could have used more violence, but we had to be careful not to kill him."

"So you burned him with cigarettes instead?"

"That is right. It is an effective method when dealing with women or very sick men."

Don controlled his rising anger, and had to make an effort to keep his expression mild and interested. He wanted to jump across the room and smash his fist into Matzka's face, but he knew that wasn't the way to play this hand.

"We have wandered from the subject of my call," Natzka went on. "The package, please, Mr. Micklem."

"I must talk to Tregarth first," Don said. "Suppose we meet again to-morrow? I'll be clearer in my mind about it after I have heard Tregarth's version. And now, signor Natzka, perhaps you will excuse me? I have still a number of things to do."

Don rose to his feet. Immediately he received a violent blow on his shoulder from behind that staggered him. He half turned to find Busso's snarling face confronting him. The automatic pointed directly between Don's eyes.

"Sit down!" Busso said, "unless you want me to hit you again."

"Yes, please sit down, Mr. Micklem," Natzka urged. "I apologize for the violence, but you don't seem to understand your position. You are my prisoner."

"Is that right?" Don said, rubbing his shoulder and grimacing. He sat down again. "You can hardly expect me to take you seriously. This is my house . . ."

"That will be remedied in a few moments, Mr. Micklem, unless, of course, you decide to co-operate. If you don't, then I shall have you removed to my own ground. But I hope that won't be necessary." Natzka took out a leather cigarette case, selected a cigarette and lit it. "You said just now that you wanted to talk to Tregarth. I'm afraid that won't be possible. Tregarth is dead."

Don looked at him; the cold grey eyes made him suddenly uneasy.

"He isn't dead," he said. "I'm afraid that bluff won't work."

"He died two minutes after you lost sight of the gondola," Natzka returned quietly. "You had no hope of getting him to hospital. I realized he must have told you where he had hidden the package. It was obvious to me that you went to get it, otherwise you would have gone with him to the hospital. My friend Dr. Vergellesi told me you planned to take Tregarth to the hospital by gondola. I had a fast motor-boat waiting. The motor-boat rammed the gondola and Tregarth was drowned. I'm afraid Mr. Micklem, you don't appreciate the size, the ramifications or the power of my organization. We have many sympathizers. We have many people who form a vast unseen army who will obey orders blindly."

Don sat motionless, his fists clenched.

"Your two colleagues made a splendid attempt to save him," Natzka went on. "I saw the whole thing myself before I came on here. But the shock of falling into the water was too much for him. If you should be worrying about your colleagues, please don't do so. They swam to the *molo* bringing Tregarth's body with them. Some of my men helped them on to the bank. Your friends quite naturally mistook them for a group of tourists until it was too late. At the moment they are quite safe in a cellar of a house not far from here: they may not be so safe if you continue to be unco-operative. So you see, Mr. Micklem, I hold all the cards. May I have the package, please?"

For a long moment Don stared at Natzka without seeing him. He was thinking of Hilda Tregarth. The British authorities had seemed convinced that Tregarth had turned traitor. The only hope of clearing him lay in the green oilskin package. If he could believe Natzka, what the package contained must be convincing proof that Tregarth had worked to the end for his country. If Don tamely handed over the package, he was destroying any hope that Hilda Tregarth might have of proving her husband's innocence.

He thought of the package lying in the copper bowl in the hall: as unsafe a place of concealment as you could choose. They had only to use their brains. They would search him, then they must realize that as the package wasn't on him he must have hidden it in the hall in the few seconds that he had had to himself before Natzka came to the study door.

He felt the palms of his hands grow moist as he saw how easily Natzka could regain the package, and he cursed himself for walking so blindly into the trap. He should have guessed Curizo and Hans wouldn't have given in so tamely unless they knew Natzka was waiting for him.

"Mr. Micklem," Natzka said sharply, "the package, please!"

"If I had it," Don said quietly, "I wouldn't give it to you, but as I haven't got it, I can't very well make an issue of it, can I?"

"I've wasted enough time already," Natzka said coldly and got to his feet. "Give me the package!"

"It's no use getting hot under the collar," Don returned mildly. "I haven't got it."

Natzka looked over at the blond man.

"Search him!"

Busso moved forward. He put his gun against the back of Don's neck.

"Get up!"

Shrugging, Don got to his feet.

102

The blond man quickly ran his hands through Don's pockets. He stepped back, shaking his head.

At this moment, the door opened and Curizo came in. He looked at Don, his dark eyes glittering, and he smiled, showing small white teeth.

"Did you keep him in sight all the time?" Natzka snapped.

"Yes. He went to a wall shrine in the calle dei Fabori. He took something from it, and when he saw me he ran away."

"Did Tregarth ever go near this wall shrine?" Natzka asked sharply.

Curizo shook his head.

"No, but the girl, Louisa Peccati did."

"That is right," Busso broke in. "Two days ago I saw her standing before the shrine. I thought she was worshipping."

"Did il signor Micklem have a chance to hide the package after he had run from the shrine?" Natzka demanded.

"No," Curizo said, "Hans and I did not let him out of our sight."

Natzka turned to Don.

"Give me the package!"

"You're not getting it," Don said quietly.

Natzka stubbed out his cigarette, then lit another. His sun-tanned face was now tight and strained. He blew smoke down his thin nostrils.

"Listen, Micklem, you still don't seem to understand your position. No one is going to stand in my way. I must have that package! I will exchange it for the lives of your two colleagues. I don't know how much you value their lives, but that is my offer. I will give you two minutes to decide. Give me the package and they will go free. Refuse, and I will give orders for both of them to be shot! I'm not bluffing. I mean exactly what I say."

Don hadn't expected this. He had imagined Natzka was going to torture him as he had tortured Tregarth, and he had made up his mind nothing Natzka did to him would make him give up the package, but this proposition was entirely different. He couldn't sacrifice Harry's and Guiseppe's lives for the honour of a dead man. But before he gave in, he was determined to make sure Natzka wasn't bluffing.

"Why should I accept your word?" he asked. "How do I know you have these two? How do I know Tregarth is dead? I'm certainly not going to give you the package until I have seen Mason and my gondolier for myself."

Natzka smiled.

"You shall see them, my friend, and what is more, unless you hand over the package you shall see them shot. You will come with me. I wouldn't advise you to attempt to escape. You are not likely to succeed, but even if you did, your two colleagues would be immediately put to death."

"I'm not going to run away," Don said. "Where are they?"

"Not far from here. Let us go."

Natzka crossed the room and went out into the hall. Don followed him with Busso and Curizo close on his heels.

Don's heart suddenly skipped a beat when he saw Natzka had paused in the middle of the hall and was looking around, an alert expression in his eyes.

"Wait a minute," he said. "All this may be entirely unnecessary. You had no chance of getting rid of the package between the shrine and this house. But you did have a few seconds alone here before I came out of the study. As the package is not on you, it isn't unreasonable to assume you hid it somewhere here."

Don's heart sank, but he kept his face expressionless.

"If you must know," he said, "I handed the package to a friend of mine in the crowd. Neither of your thugs spotted me giving it to him, and he was bright enough not to ask questions. Unless Mason and my gondolier are set free you haven't a hope of getting it back."

Natzka looked sharply at Curizo.

"Could he have done that without you seeing him?"

Curizo hesitated, then nodded.

"Yes. The crowd was very dense. He wasn't ever out of our sight, but we could see only his head and shoulders. I couldn't see what he was doing with his hands. He could have given it to someone."

"Very clever of you, Mr. Micklem," Natzka said, his smile brittle. "But that really doesn't alter the situation. You will get the package from your friend and you will give it to me."

"I must be certain first that you have Mason and Guiseppe," Don said, beginning to breathe again.

"Yes, you shall see them." Natzka looked around the hall again. "And yet..." He broke off and smiled at Don. "This friend of yours in the crowd could be a figment of your imagination, of course. Why should you tell me about him if you weren't trying to divert my attention? I think we will examine the hall before we go." He looked over at Busso. "Shoot him if he moves!" Then he turned to Curizo. "See if you can find it. He hadn't much time. It'll be in an accessible place. Brun, look around," he went on as the blond man came to the study door.

Don mentally shrugged his shoulders. Luck was against him. He had done his best, but now they were certain to find the package. What will happen to Harry and Guiseppe? He wondered. What is going to happen to me? These thugs haven't hesitated to murder Louisa Peccati. They might think it a good idea to silence the three of us in the same way.

He watched the two men searching the hall. He saw Curizo was getting near the copper pot. He remembered the game called "hot and cold" he used to play when he was a kid, and he felt the same anxious excitement now as he used to feel when one of the seekers was close to the place where he had hidden the object to be found.

Curizo suddenly picked up the pot. Don's heart skipped a beat as Curizo turned the pot upside down. Nothing fell out of it.

With sick relief, mingled with bewilderment, Don realized the copper pot was now as empty as a hole in a wall.

At the end of an extensive five minutes' searching, Curizo said, "It is not in the hall."

Natzka shrugged his shoulders.

"I should have been surprised if it had been, but it was worth a try. Then your story, Mr. Micklem, about your friend seems to be true."

Don touched his dry lips with the tip of his tongue. He realized he was now in a jam. He hadn't any doubt that if he didn't hand over the package, Natzka would carry out his threat to shoot both Harry and Guiseppe. Where was the package? Who had taken it? Was it Curizo? He had come in some minutes after Don had gone into the study; he had had the hall to himself. Was Curizo planning to do a private deal with the package, double-crossing Natzka? It must have been Curizo who had taken it!

Natzka said, "Let us go, Mr. Micklem. You shall see your colleagues, then you will go to this friend of yours and collect the package."

"Just a moment," Don said. He realized that if Curizo had taken the package and once he was allowed to leave the house and hide the package somewhere, there would be no way of proving he had taken it. Don saw his only hope was to catch Curizo with the package on him.

"Well, what is it?" Natzka asked impatiently.

"I was kidding about the friend," Don said. "You were right: I did hide the package here."

While he spoke, Don was watching Curizo, but the lean, swarthy face showed only surprise.

"That is interesting," Natzka said. "Why tell me that? You are discarding your bargaining powers, Mr. Micklem."

"I've lost them, anyway," Don said quietly. "When I came in, and before you showed up, I put the package in that copper pot."

Natzka looked at the pot, then at Curizo who went over to the pot again. He looked inside and, picking it up, he turned it upside down.

"There's nothing in it," he said unnecessarily.

"If this is a device to waste time, Mr. Micklem," Natzka said, an edge to his voice, "it is a poor one, and one you may regret."

"I put the package in the pot," Don said. "Someone has taken it while we were in the study. There was only one person who came into the hall while we were in the study, and that's this guy here," and he nodded at Curizo.

Curizo stiffened, his lips coming off his teeth in an angry snarl.

"If you are trying to stir up trouble among my men you won't succeed," Natzka said curtly. "It is too old a trick. We will go and see your friends. I have no doubt I will be able to persuade you to hand over the package when the right moment comes."

Busso dug his gun into Don's spine.

"Move!" he said.

"Someone took the package," Don repeated, holding his ground. "The most likely person is Curizo. Before we go, you'd better have him searched. I wouldn't mind betting he has the package on him."

Curizo took two quick steps forward and slapped Don heavily across his face with his open hand, sending him staggering back. Busso's gun poked against his spine, reminding him not to start anything.

"Carrion!" Curizo snarled.

"Get away from him!" Natzka barked. His face was hard and his grey eyes were suspicious. As Curizo reluctantly stepped away, Natzka went on, "That was a dangerous thing to have said, my friend. Curizo has a habit of harbouring a grudge."

"Search him," Don said. "Don't be a mug, Natzka. Why should you trust him? If he found the package and thought he could make something out of it, why do you imagine he would hand it over to you?"

Natzka's eyes alerted. He looked sharply at the snarling Curizo.

"Did you find the package?" he asked softly.

"No! He's lying!" Curizo said furiously. "See for yourself!"

He began to turn out his pockets, throwing the few articles he was carrying on the floor. He pulled out the insides of his pockets, his face contorted with rage.

"Now are you satisfied?"

"Better make sure he isn't wearing a belt," Don said, trying to sound calmer than he felt.

"See if he is wearing a belt," Natzka said to Brun who approached Curizo apologetically. He ran his hands over Curizo as if he were stroking a tiger.

"There is nothing," he said, stepping back.

"Well?" Natzka said, looking at Don.

"He could have hidden it somewhere," Don said.

"Do you think so? Do you know what I think? You are trying to create a diversion. Well, Mr. Micklem, you have brought this on yourself," Natzka said. "The matter could have been arranged without any unpleasantness, but now, it is due to Curizo to handle it as he thinks fit." He turned to Curizo. "I am returning to the hotel. I want that package within two hours from now. I will leave the finding of it to you."

"Yes," Curizo said between his teeth. He looked at Don, a tight, cruel smile lighting his face. "You shall have it within two hours."

"Good." Natzka turned to Don. "You shouldn't have interfered. I am sorry, but you must now suffer for your foolishness. You will be taken to the house where your friends are. You will be persuaded to hand over the package. I have warned you before not to attempt to escape." He went to the door, opened it and turned to smile at Don. "I will say good-bye. It is very unlikely that we shall meet again."

"For your sake I hope we don't," Don said evenly.

Natzka shrugged.

"That kind of bravado doesn't impress me," he said. "Goodbye, Mr. Micklem."

He crossed the hall, and a moment later they heard the front door shut.

The gondola edged up to the mooring-post outside a dilapidated house, shrouded in darkness, in one of the narrow *rii* behind the Ghetto Nuovo.

Brun tied up the gondola and stepped on to the small landing-stage.

"Get out!" Curizo said to Don.

Don climbed out on to the landing-stage and looked quickly to right and left. The *rio* was dark, and he could see nothing, but his sharp ears told him that not far off another gondola was coming down the *rio*.

Curizo heard it, too, for taking Don by the arm he hustled him through a doorway into evil-smelling darkness.

Busso and Brun followed and closed the door.

Busso stepped close to Don, holding his gun against Don's side.

Curizo struck a match and lit a candle. He walked down a narrow passage, pushed open a door and began to descend steep, dirty stairs.

Busso shoved Don forward, and Don went down the stairs into a big damp cellar lit by three flickering candles stuck in bottles on a big wooden case.

Sitting on the floor, their backs to the wall, their hands and feet roped, were Harry and Guiseppe.

Don looked at them and grimaced. He had hoped that Natzka had been bluffing, but the sight of these two now underlined the jam he was in.

"Hello, boss," Harry said. "Sorry about this. We played our hand badly."

Harry looked in a bad way. His eye had now turned black. Down one side of his face was a deep scratch that had dripped blood on to his collar and shoulder. His clothes were wet and torn.

Guiseppe was in no better state. He had a gash on his forehead, and his face was bloodstained, but he managed a smile as Don met his eyes.

"Shut up!" Brun said to Harry and walking over to him, he kicked him savagely in the ribs, sending him over on his side.

Don restrained himself with an effort. Busso's gun kept grinding into his side. He had no doubt that Busso would shoot him if he did make a hostile move.

Curizo pulled up a chair and set it in the middle of the cellar by the lighted candles.

"Sit down!" he snarled.

Don sat down.

Busso moved away and leaned against the wall, gun in hand.

"Hold him," Curizo said to Brun who came up behind Don, grabbed his wrists and jerked his arms behind the chair in an agonizing grip.

Curizo stood before Don, his swarthy face cold and vicious.

"So you tried to make trouble for me," he said softly. "No one does that without paying for it." He took from his hip pocket a stained, sweat-darkened kid glove which he put on his right hand. He flexed his fingers, then closed his fist.

Don watched him narrowly, his muscles tense. Although he couldn't move his body, he could move his head, and he waited ready to duck.

"I'm going to give you a beating," Curizo said softly. "Like this . . ."

His fist flashed at Don's face. Don shifted his head a fraction of an inch and the gloved fist scraped past his ear, making Curizo come forward, off balance. Don hooked his foot around Curizo's ankle and jerked. Curizo sprawled on the floor near where Harry was lying. Harry kicked at his face, but Curizo just managed to roll out of reach.

Busso stepped up to Don and hit him on the side of his jaw with his gun barrel. Don jerked his head back, riding most of the savage blow, but not all of it.

Momentarily stunned, he was vaguely aware that Curizo had got to his feet.

Cursing, Curizo caught hold of Don's hair, jerked his head back, and raised his fist to smash it down on Don's face, but Busso caught his wrist.

"No!" Busso said. "He's got to see his friend. Don't mark him."

Curizo wrenched his wrist free and stepped back, his eyes glittering and his mouth working. For a moment he struggled to control himself, then he seemed to realize the sense of what Busso had said and he turned away, muttering.

"Are you going to get that package?" Busso said to Don.

His face throbbing, and still a little dazed, Don realized none of these thugs would believe him if he told them he had no idea where the package was. He could tell by Curizo's white, murderous face that he would shoot either Harry or Guiseppe if he should show the slightest hesitation. Curizo had already pulled an automatic from a shoulder holster and was looking towards Harry who had struggled up into a sitting position.

Don realized their only chance was to play for time.

"I'll get it," he said.

Curizo showed his teeth.

"Where is it?"

"My friend is staying at the Londra Hotel," Don said.

"His name?"

"Jack Montgomery," Don said, remembering just in time that one of his club associates was staying at the Londra.

Curizo turned to Brun.

"Telephone the hotel and find out if such a man is staying there."

Brun went up the stairs.

Curizo paced up and down until Brun came back.

"There is such a man. He is in the hotel now," he said.

Curizo looked at Don.

"You will get the package. Busso and Brun will go with you. If you make a false move, these two will be shot. I will personally shoot them. Do you understand?"

"Yes," Don said.

"Take him," Curizo said to Busso. "Wait outside the hotel for him. If he doesn't come out in ten minutes send Brun back here to tell me."

"Come on," Busso said to Don. He waved his gun in Don's face.

Don got unsteadily to his feet. He looked over at Harry and Guiseppe. Both of them were staring at him anxiously, but Harry managed a grin.

"Don't worry about us, boss," he said.

"I'll be back," Don said, but as he climbed the stairs he desperately tried to think of a way out of this jam. His only hope now was to surprise these two, lay them out, and come back to surprise Curizo, but Busso seemed alert to such a move. His gun never left off digging into Don's spine, and Don knew so long as the gun was in that position, he couldn't make a hostile move.

At the head of the stairs, Busso caught hold of Don's arm.

"Wait," he said. "Go and see if there is anyone about," he went on to Brun.

Brun pushed past Don, went down the passage, and Don heard him open the front door.

Busso, his gun still pressing into Don's ribs, waited. There was a long pause.

Don could hear Busso's heavy breathing. He was very tempted to jump aside and attempt to close with Busso, but he realized it would be a suicidal move. The best time to start trouble, he decided, was when they were getting into the gondola. If he could catch them off balance and tip them into the water . . .

Brun's voice came out of the darkness: "It is all right."

"Move!" Busso said, stabbing at Don's back with the gun.

Don went forward into the darkness. Through the open doorway ahead of him, he could just make out the gleam of stars above the dark outline of roofs.

Busso's gun was poking into his ribs as he stepped on to the landing stage. He saw Brun standing by the wall. Then he saw a second shadowy figure a split second before Busso saw it.

Something that glittered in the starlight flashed past Don, and he heard Busso catch his breath in a sharp grunt of pain. The gun ceased to press into Don's side. He spun around as he heard the gun drop to the ground.

Busso was bent double, clutching his arm. Don hit him a crushing punch on the side of his jaw.

Busso sagged at the knees, then slid down and spread out on the ground.

Brun started forward, then stopped.

Cherry's fruity voice said, "Don't you dare move, my man!"

"Cherry!" Don gasped. "Well, I'll be damned!"

"Yes, sir," Cherry said calmly. "Should I pass my sword through this fellow?"

"Your sword?" Don gasped. "Have you got a sword?"

"Yes, sir. I think I mentioned my swordstick to you."

"Don't kill him," Don said, his voice suddenly shaking with laughter. "I'll handle him."

He stepped up to Brun, swept aside Brun's hesitant guard, and slammed a punch to his jaw, driving him on to his hands and knees.

"I have a cosh here, sir," Cherry said gravely, "if you would care to use it. It's a weapon I would rather not handle myself if you don't mind."

111

He handed Don a short, lead-loaded cane.

Don took it and struck Brun on the head with it just as Brun half struggled up.

Brun gave a strangled grunt and spread out on top of Busso.

# CHAPTER TEN

*At All Costs ...*

---

"THAT appears, sir, to be quite a scientific process," Cherry said, bending to peer at Brun's prostrate form. "Personally, I should be nervous of fracturing his skull."

Don leaned weakly against the wall. Cherry's sudden appearance was so unexpected, his pompous manner so unruffled that Don didn't know whether to burst out laughing or throw his arms around Cherry's neck.

"Harry and Guiseppe are in trouble in there," he said. "I'll get them out; then you can tell me where you've sprung from. You wait here and keep a look-out."

He bent and groped on the landing-stage until he found Busso's gun.

"Perhaps you would care for me to come with you, sir?" Cherry asked.

"No. You wait here and watch these two." Don handed back the cosh. "If they move, hit them and hit them hard. Don't worry about breaking their skulls."

"If you say so, sir."

Don re-entered the house, moved silently along the dark passage and paused at the head of the stairs to listen. He could hear Curizo moving about in the cellar.

He began to descend the stairs, keeping close to the wall, treading carefully, testing each stair for a creak before putting his weight on it.

Half-way down, he could see into the cellar.

Curizo was pacing up and down, his hands in his trousers pockets.

Don smiled grimly. Curizo was about to have the shock of his life.

He leaned over the banister rail, his gun pointing at Curizo.

"Don't start anything funny," he said quietly.

Curizo jumped as if he had been shot. He began to take his hands out of his pockets, but seeing the gun pointing at him, he froze into motionlessness, his lips coming off his teeth in a snarl of fury.

"It didn't work, pal," Don said. "Now it's my turn to get rough."

"Nice work, boss," Harry said happily. "I knew you'd pull it off."

"Stay as you are," Don went on to Curizo. "I'm itching to shoot you, so if you're tired of life, start something funny."

Curizo stood still, his eyes smouldering, his mouth twitching.

Don came down the stairs, slowly step by step, his eyes never leaving Curizo.

"Turn around," he said.

"I'll make you pay for this!" Curizo snarled.

"Turn around!"

Slowly Curizo turned. Don reversed the gun, now holding it by its barrel. He stepped softly up to Curizo and slammed the butt of the gun down on top of his head.

Curizo grunted, his knees hinged and he flopped to the floor. Don knew he wouldn't have to hit him again. The jar that had run up his arm as the butt encountered Curizo's skull told him Curizo would be out for a long time.

"Good shot, boss," Harry exclaimed. "How did you fix those other two?"

Don went over to him, took out his pocket-knife and slashed through the ropes that bound him.

"It was Cherry," he said. "The old boy was hiding on the landing-stage, complete with a swordstick and a cosh. He was terrific!"

"Cherry?" Harry gasped, getting unsteadily to his feet. "How did he know we were here?"

"He'll tell us," Don said, freeing Guiseppe. "How are you two feeling?"

"Wet and horrible," Harry said, grinning.

"I am all right, signore," Guiseppe said, struggling to his feet. "But I am glad you came back. That man Curizo is bad."

"An understatement," Don said, smiling, "but never mind." He suddenly remembered Tregarth. In the excitement Tregarth had gone out of his mind. "What happened to Tregarth, Harry? Natzka said he died."

"I'm afraid that's right. We hadn't a chance. The motor-boat caught us as we were turning a corner into another *rio*. I thought it was an accident. We both did what we could for him, but he was pretty bad as you know, and the shock of falling into the water finished him. Five or six men, got up as American tourists, helped us out. We were right off our guard. All we

114

could think of was Mr. Tregarth. I just had time to make sure he was dead when I was hit on the head. I woke up here."

"Poor devil," Don said. "You don't know what happened to his body?"

"I heard one of them say something about burying him out at sea," Harry said, rubbing his aching wrists. "They seemed anxious his body shouldn't be found."

"You're quite sure he was dead?"

"Yes, boss, there was no doubt about it."

"All right. Come on, we can't afford to waste any time. We'll bring those two thugs down here and rope the three of them up. We have two hours before Natzka begins to wonder what has happened. There's a lot to be done in those two hours."

It didn't take the four of them long to get Busso and Brun down into the cellar. Harry set about roping them while Don tied Curizo up.

While they were doing this, Cherry sat on the chair, nursing his swordstick while he regained his breath.

"Come on, Cherry, tell us what happened," Don said, busy roping Curizo's ankles. "How did you get back so fast?"

"I went to the hotel in Paris as you told me to, sir," Cherry said. "I ascertained that the man who had telephoned you was not Mr. Tregarth. This man had left the hotel, but he had left a message for you. In the note, he said he was in serious danger and was leaving for Brussells. He gave the name of a hotel there and asked you to follow him immediately."

"I imagined that was the idea," Don said. "A wild goose-chase all over Europe while Natzka was free to do what he liked here."

"Yes, sir," Cherry went on, "I decided I might be more useful if I returned immediately. I was fortunate to catch a fast plane back to Milan, and from there I chartered a plane to the Lido. I returned to the *palazzo* and went to my room. A few minutes later I heard strange voices in the hall and I went to investigate. I found three men with guns, holding up the rest of the staff. They didn't see me, and deciding the odds were a little too heavy for me, I concealed myself in a cupboard."

The idea of fat Cherry hiding in a cupboard appealed to Harry.

"Well, you couldn't call it the skeleton in the cupboard, could you?" he said, grinning.

Cherry gave him a cold, distant stare, and went on, "They sent a man with the staff into the kitchen, and then this Natzka person went into the lounge. I was about to telephone for the police when I heard you come in. I had no time to warn you. I observed you put something in the copper bowl . . ."

"Have you got it, Cherry?" Don asked eagerly.

"Yes, sir. I listened outside the door and heard Natzka ask you for the package. I realized the hiding-place wasn't safe, so I took the liberty of removing the package."

"And you've got it?"

Cherry produced the green oilskin package from his pocket and gave it to Don.

"You will find it quite intact, sir."

"Well done! You did exactly right."

"Thank you, sir. I waited outside the house, and followed you when you came out. I had a little trouble in borrowing a gondola, and still more trouble in handling it, but I was fortunate to come across their gondola moored outside this house. I waited on the landing-stage, and when the man came out, I threatened him with my sword, and he surrendered."

Don grinned.

"You deserve the Order of Merit, Cherry," he said, as he satisfied himself that the three men were now securely tied. "Let's get out of here. Guiseppe, you take their gondola and lose it. Go home and wait instructions. You two come with me. We'll go back to the *palazzo*."

He led the way quickly up the stairs, followed by the others.

In less than twenty minutes, Don, changed and once more his usual spruce self, sat down in his study to examine the oilskin package while outside in the hall both Harry and Cherry kept guard.

Don slit open the package and carefully unrolled the oilskin. Into his hand dropped a small leather-bound book: not more than three inches square. Folded around the book and secured by an elastic band was a sealed envelope addressed to Hilda Tregarth and several sheets of soiled notepaper, covered with neat, small handwriting that Don recognized as the handwriting he had seen on the postcard of the Bridge of Sighs. He glanced inside the book. Apart from the first page that contained a mass of symbols and figures of some complicated code, the rest of the book contained blank pages. He dropped the book into his pocket, then opened up the sheets of notepaper. He saw the letter was addressed to himself, and glancing at the last page, saw the signature: John Tregarth.

He reached for a cigar, lit it, and settling down in his chair, began to read.

*Dear Micklem,*

*By the time this letter reaches you, if it ever does reach you, it will be most unlikely that I shall still be alive. I am writing this in an empty house in the calle Mondello. I am in a pretty bad way, and my only hope of getting this to you is through Louisa Peccati who has done everything she can to help me.*

*The leather-bound book, you will find with this letter, is of vital importance to the British Government. I can't tell you what it contains, but every effort will be made by Natzka, an enemy of my country, to regain it. It has been stolen by me from his organization and I am giving it to you to get back at all costs to Sir Robert Graham. I had no idea what I was going to do with the book, ill and trapped as I am, until I saw in the newspaper that you were coming to Venice. I then remembered how you handled the plane during that run to Rome and how unperturbed you were when things got hot. If anyone can get this book back to England, you can. I am asking you to get it back not only because of its vital importance to my country, but also because of Hilda who has been led to believe I have turned traitor.*

*The only way I could get at the book was to pretend to go over to the "other side". Sir Robert assisted me in doing this. So important was it that they shouldn't suspect me, my wife hasn't been told. No one but Sir Robert, you and I know the truth, but now, it doesn't matter, and I am relying on you to tell my wife and to put her mind at rest.*

*About the book; whatever you do, don't do the obvious. Don't go to the British Consul with it. Don't put it into the post. You must deliver the book into Sir Robert's own hands and no one else's. These people have agents everywhere, and they would think nothing of tampering with the mails. Trust no one. If Natzka suspects you have the book he won't hesitate to wipe you out. Don't underestimate this mission. You will have great difficulty in leaving Italy. Every means will be made to prevent you going. The opposition will follow you across France. What you must constantly keep in mind is there are many officials working for Natzka and what he stands for; the police, the customs men, men at the airports, innkeepers, petrol attendants will have instructions to put your car out of action, crash the plane you are in, arrest you*

117

*on some pretext on a train. You cannot be too careful, and
your task is almost impossible. I'm telling you this so you do
not underestimate the opposition.*

*I spent five nightmare weeks getting out of Vienna, and I
know the dodges they get up to. If they once suspect you
have the book, you won't have a safe second until you hand it
to Sir Robert. I am sorry to land you in this mess, but you
are my only hope. I know I can rely on you to do your best.
The enclosed letter is for Hilda. Will you try to get it to her?
It may help to soften the shock of not seeing me again.*

*Good luck and good hunting.*

*John Tregarth.*

Don turned the sealed envelope over between his fingers as
he stared down at the polished top of his desk. His mind was
busy. He glanced at his wrist-watch. He had a clear hour before
Natzka would begin to wonder what Curizo was up to.

He did not hesitate to take up Tregarth's challenge. The pros-
pects of the journey ahead of him gave him a feeling of excitement. He got to his feet, stubbed out his cigar before crossing the
room to open the study door.

"Harry!"

"Yes, boss," Harry said, coming away from the front door.

"Go to Guiseppe as fast as you can, tell him to have the
motor-boat ready for a trip to the Lido. Tell him I want the
tanks filled to capacity. Fast and urgent, Harry!"

Harry nodded, opened the front door and went quickly away
into the darkness.

Don turned to Cherry.

"Get a couple of rucksacks and pack them for a week's camp-
ing. You know what I usually take. Organize some food and
brandy, and let's have some action."

"Very good, sir," Cherry said, his eyes showing his excitement. He went off down the passage at a surprising pace.

Don ran upstairs, threw off his lounge suit and put on a wool
open-neck shirt, a pair of dark brown slacks and a leather wind-
cheater. He stowed the little book that had come to him from
Tregarth in a body belt he put on under his shirt.

Moving quickly, he took a small automatic from his dressing-
table drawer and slipped it into his hip pocket. From a box in
the same drawer he took five additional clips of ammunition
which he carried downstairs to where Cherry was waiting, rucksacks ready.

"I'm going back to London, Cherry," Don said as he stowed the ammunition in one of the rucksacks. "If anyone asks for me, tell them I am in Rome on business, and I expect to be back at the end of the week."

"Very good, sir. You're sure you wouldn't like me to come with you?" Cherry asked, his fat face showing his disappointment.

"I want you to stay here and look after things. Harry will be with me."

Harry himself appeared in the front doorway.

"All okay, boss. Guiseppe is filling the tanks now. She'll be ready when you are."

"Get into something that'll stand wear, Harry," Don said. "Snap it up! We may have some hiking to do."

Harry grinned cheerfully.

"Okay, boss," and he bolted up the stairs.

Don went into his study and rang up the airport. The time was now ten minutes after midnight. So much had happened since he had seen Stefano Peccati that it seemed incredible to him more time hadn't passed.

A brisk voice answered his call, and he asked to be connected with Pleydell.

"I'm sorry, signore, but il signor Pleydell is not here."

"Where can I find him?"

"I do not know, signore."

"This is Don Micklem speaking," Don said. "I want to charter a plane immediately for Paris. Can you fix that?"

"I will see. Will you hold on a moment?"

Don waited impatiently. After a long delay, the voice said, "I am afraid we have no private charter planes available until noon to-morrow."

"I don't care what it costs. I've got to fly to Paris to-night," Don snapped.

"I'm afraid that won't be possible, signore," the voice said. "The earliest is noon to-morrow."

"Connect me to the airport manager," Don said curtly.

"He has gone home, signore."

There was a flat note of unco-operation in the voice that warned Don he was merely wasting time. He wondered bleakly if there were planes to be had and whether this was the work of the organization Tregarth had warned him about. Surely they couldn't have got into action so soon?

He hung up, opened his desk drawer and took out a bundle

119

of large-scale maps of the country he always kept handy. Then he went briskly into the hall.

Harry, dressed more or less the same way now as Don was, was waiting for him.

"We're leaving for London right away," Don said. "We're up against tough opposition. These thugs will stop at nothing to prevent us getting out of the country. I'm not going to risk taking the train. I think a car is too dangerous. I can't get a plane so we'll go by boat. We'll head for Chioggia, then down to the mouth of the Po, then up river as far as Piacenza. We'll leave the boat there, and try for a plane at Milan."

Harry grimaced.

"That'll take time, boss."

"Yes, but I don't think they'll imagine that's the way we'll go. They'll watch the road and the airports. With any luck they won't think of the river. Come on; let's go."

Cherry came forward.

"If there's anything I can do, sir . . ."

Don grinned at him.

"You've done more than your share. The rest is up to us. I'll be seeing you in a week. If I'm not back here by then, shut up the house and come home."

Although it was after midnight, the quay was still crowded with tourists, and Don and Harry had trouble in making speed towards the boat station where Guiseppe was waiting for them.

Eventually they forced their way through the crowd and up a narrow *calle* which opened into a boat basin where private owners kept their motor-boats.

"What's up now?" Harry muttered as they heard Guiseppe's voice raised in anger. "Sounds like he's cursing someone."

They could just make out in the dim light of the overhead lamp, Guiseppe standing by Don's thirty-two foot cabin cruisette, shaking his fist into the face of a fat man in dirty overalls who kept spreading his hands and shrugging his shoulders, indifferent to Guiseppe's cursing.

"What's the trouble?" Don asked sharply, coming up beside Guiseppe.

"This son of a pig says he has no petrol, signore," Guiseppe snarled. "He always has petrol. He is too lazy to unlock the pump."

The fat man turned to bow to Don.

"It is unfortunate, signore, but I have run out of petrol. This stupid gondolier will not believe me. To-morrow, a new delivery arrives. Then I shall be only too glad to supply il signore."

"What have we got in the tanks, Joe?" Don asked.

"One tank is empty, signore; the other is half full."

Harry had quietly walked behind the fat man and was examining the pump. He gave the tank a gentle kick. From the dull response he knew the tank must be full.

"He's lying, boss," he said. "There's all the gas we want in here."

The fat man turned savagely on Harry and exploded into a stream of Italian invective. Since Harry didn't know a word of Italian, the effort was wasted on him.

Don gave Guiseppe a signal and Guiseppe's lips parted in a happy smile. He closed his great fist and brought it down on top of the fat man's head. Harry obligingly stepped forward and caught the fat man as he slumped forward and laid him gently on the cobblestones.

"Get his keys and get the pump working," Don said, hurriedly stepping into the boat. "Joe, take this man out of sight and sit on him until we've gone. Here, take this and pay him." He thrust some lira bills into Guiseppe's hand. "You'll probably be able to scare him into keeping his mouth shut."

"I will scare him all right, signore," Guiseppe said grimly. "There is nothing further I can do for il signore?"

"No, and thanks a lot, Joe."

Guiseppe picked up the fat man, slung him over his shoulder and walked off with him into the darkness.

First the plane, now petrol, Don was thinking. Too much of a coincidence not to be engineered. It looked as if Natzka had taken precautions to stop him leaving, on the off-chance he might escape.

With the tanks full, Harry stepped down into the boat and started the engine.

"Take it easy until we get out into the lagoon," Don told him, "then let her rip."

As the boat nosed its way down the narrow *rio*, they heard the sound of running footsteps.

"What's this? More trouble?" Harry muttered and pushed forward the throttle slightly, increasing speed. They both looked back over their shoulders.

Two policemen appeared out of the shadows.

"Hey, you there! Bring that boat back!" one of them shouted.

"Shall we stop, boss?"

"Slow down, but keep her moving," Don said quietly, "and be ready to let her go if I tell you."

He stood up as the two policemen came abreast of the boat.

"What's the trouble?" he called.

"Bring that boat to the side!"

"What's the idea?"

"You know what the idea is. You've just stolen a load of gasoline," one of the policemen shouted. "Bring her to the side."

Don smiled.

"Sorry, but I'm in a hurry." He realized that once he got into the hands of the police the delay of explaining would be endless. This could easily be another attempt to keep him in Venice. "Let her rip, Harry."

Harry opened the throttle and the boat swept forward.

"Keep your head down!" Don said. "They're going to shoot."

One of the policemen had unslung his carbine, but before he could get it to his shoulder, Harry had swung the now fast-moving boat around the corner into a broader *rio,* and, seeing an empty stretch of water ahead of him, he pushed the throttle wide open.

With a roar from the powerful engines, the prow of the boat lifted clear of the water, and the boat surged forward at its full racing speed.

Twenty minutes later, with the engines going at half-speed, they swept past the Lido landing-stage and headed towards Pellestrina.

Don crouched over the powerful short-wave radio receiver, headphones clamped over his ears, his fingers on the tuning knob.

Harry, cigarette between his lips, his eyes alert, sat at the helm. He was thoroughly enjoying himself. It was some time now since he had had any excitement, and he was ripe for it.

Don gave a sudden shrug, took off the headphones, reached for a cigarette and lit it. He turned around in the bucket seat so he could face Harry.

"We're not going to get far in this tub, Harry," he said. "The police of all coast towns as far as Rimini are being warned to look out for us. The Chioggia police have two motor-boats in the gulf, looking for us."

"They've got nothing that could catch us, boss," Harry said.

"That's not the point," Don said. "It was a smart move to force us to take the gasoline. We've now got the whole of the Italian police on our necks. They'll do Natzka's work for him, and it means the whole country in a little while will be on the look-out for us. This boat sticks out a mile: the biggest dope would recognize it once a description of it gets going, and they're burning up the ether already. We'll never be able to take it up the Po without being recognized. If it wasn't for those two police boats in the gulf I'd have a shot at making Trieste, but the risk is too great. I guess our safest move is to head for the mainland, leave the boat and try to get to Padova on foot. Those two policemen couldn't have got a clear enough view of us to describe what we're wearing. We stand a better chance without the boat."

Harry nodded.

"Okay, boss. Do we pull in before we reach Chioggia?"

"We'll pull in now."

Harry swung over the helm.

"Go in at quarter speed," Don said peering into the darkness. He thought he heard a distant sound. "I think there's a motor-boat somewhere around. Cut the engines!"

Harry closed the throttle and the motor-boat slowed to a crawl through the still water of the lagoon.

"Over to the right, boss," Harry muttered, "and coming fast."

The drone of powerful engines could be clearly heard now, but it was too dark to see anything.

"We'll take a chance and wait. They may pass us," Don said and hurriedly put out his cigarette.

They waited, tense and listening

"Sounds as if they are coming right on us," Harry said suddenly.

"Quarter speed to port," Don said.

The motor-boat began to move again: its powerful engine making scarcely any noise.

The drone of the approaching police boat was now turning into a steady roar. Then suddenly the dazzling white beam of a searchlight lit up the dark waters.

"It's a police boat all right," Don said. "We'll have to run, Harry. Full speed ahead!"

The searchlight swept round and lit up their boat as its nose rose out of the water and it surged forward.

"Give me the helm," Don said. "We'll run out to sea and try to lose them."

"She's got more speed than I thought," Harry said changing seats with Don.

"She's not fast enough to catch us," Don said.

As the police boat turned in a large half-circle to come after them, the beam of the searchlight lost them, and for a brief minute they fled over the water in darkness, then the beam caught them again.

"Keep down. They mustn't get a look at us," Don said, crouching himself.

"We're pulling away," Harry said.

A tiny red flash of flame showed from the following boat, then the crack of a gun followed. Something that sounded like an angry hornet zipped past overhead.

"They'll warn the other boat. We've got to watch out," Don said.

Already the beam of the searchlight was losing its effectiveness as the distance between the two speeding boats widened.

Another flash came from the following boat, and this time, the bullet thudded into the roof of the cabin, sending a shower of wood splinters into the cabin.

"Who said the Eye-ties couldn't shoot?" Harry muttered.

Don altered course, advanced the throttle slightly. The boat surged forward even faster.

The searchlight beam now no longer held them, and as if realizing its uselessness, it was suddenly turned off.

Don sent the boat around in a wide circle and headed back to the mainland.

They could see the two red lamps on the police boat a quarter of a mile now to port, moving steadily out to sea.

"I think we've foxed them," Don said, "but they'll be back."

"We can't be more than half a mile from the mainland," Harry said. "What are you going to do, boss? Run her on to the beach?"

"I guess so. We don't want to get our feet wet." Don grinned. "Unless, of course, we have to. We've a long walk ahead of us."

"They've found the other boat," Harry said, looking back.

In the far distance they could see the searchlight of the police boat had lit up the second police boat. Both boats swung in a circle and were now heading back for the mainland.

"Here they come," Harry muttered. "Surf ahead, boss."

124

Don cut down speed.

The motor-boat began to bounce on the waves that were running strongly inshore. The dark outlines of the beach loomed up before them.

"Stand by for a jar," Don said and took the boat straight in.

A few moments later they were sprinting across the wet sands towards the dark interior.

# CHAPTER ELEVEN

*Tallyho!*

---

BOTH Don and Harry were tireless walkers. They made it a matter of personal pride to keep in first-class trim, and the journey ahead presented no fears for them.

After ten minutes of plodding over rough country, they struck a road that Don's map told him would take them to Piove di Sacco.

The terrain was flat and exposed, and Don realized they would have to find some place to hide up in during the day. In daylight they would be seen for miles around, and he had no doubt that as soon as the police had discovered the abandoned boat, they would begin a systematic search of the district.

"I don't think we should make for Padova now," he said as he swung along briskly at Harry's side. "The police are certain to look out for us in the big towns. Our best plan is to keep to the villages and by-pass the towns."

"I wish we had the Bentley with us, boss," Harry said feelingly. "We'd be home in no time."

"Maybe later, when we've found out how interested the police really are in us, we can take the risk of hiring a car," Don said. "Maybe it would be safer to board a C.I.T. bus."

"This seems a pretty exposed spot. We'll have to get under cover before daylight."

"Just what I was thinking," Don said. "Keep a watch out for a farmhouse. We might be able to hole up in a barn or an outbuilding."

They had walked for perhaps twenty minutes when Don's sharp ears caught the faint sound of an approaching car.

"Hear that, Harry?"

Harry was already moving off the road. He jumped down into the ditch that ran alongside the road. Don followed him, and they crouched down, listening to the approaching hum of the car engine.

The car went past. It had only its sidelights on, and Don caught a glimpse of four men in the car, all wearing flat peak caps of the police.

"They haven't wasted much time," he said, straightening.

"Shall we leave the road and cut over the fields? It might be safer."

"Harder going, boss. I think we should stick to the road as long as we can."

"Okay; let's go then."

They regained the road and continued on their way, their eyes and ears alert for any sound.

It was twenty minutes past three by Don's luminous wristwatch before they came upon their first farmhouse.

By now, a big, white moon was lighting up the flat countryside, and they easily spotted the whitewashed walls of the farmhouse that stood in a field set back from the road.

"Shall we take a look, boss?" Harry asked, slowing down.

Don stopped and studied the farmhouse. He could make out the high roof of the barn that stood away from the house; the cowsheds and the outbuildings.

"You can bet your last buck the police have warned the farmer to look out for us. They'll have gone to all the farms on the road ahead of us. Still, there's no harm trying. We've got to get off the road before daylight. Come on; let's investigate."

They left the road and walked quietly across the field, keeping away from the rough brick cart-track that led directly to the farm.

They had got within a hundred yards of the farm when a dog began to bark.

"That's that. Come on; let's get back to the road."

"Half a mo', boss; I've got a way with dogs. I'll see if I can make friends with the fella."

"Too late," Don said. "Look . . ."

A light came up in one of the upper windows of the farmhouse. The dog began to bark more ferociously and rattle on its chain.

"Just a moment," Harry said. He had been in many tight corners during his Commando service, and he had learned the unexpected move often paid dividends. "Let's make for the barn. They might think the dog has scared us off."

Don nodded.

"Idea. Come on . . ."

Moving silently and keeping in the shadow, they ran swiftly forward and got around to the back of the barn as they heard the bolts on the farmhouse door being noisily drawn back.

A woman called out of a window: "Be careful, papa; better wait for Vittore."

"If I waited for him I would be dead and buried," a man shouted back. "Someone's worrying the dog."

"I'm coming, papa," another man shouted.

"That makes two of them," Harry muttered. "Hey-ho, papa's let the dog loose."

"Now's the time to show your talent then," Don said. "I'll leave it to you."

Harry moved forward silently. A moment later a big black dog came bounding around the barn. He gave a low growling snarl and came on towards Harry.

Don's heart skipped a beat when he saw Harry made no move to avoid the dog. Harry remained motionless; the dog hesitated, then paused to sniff cautiously at him.

"Good boy," Harry muttered and whistled softly between his teeth.

The dog came closer, then began to wag its tail and Harry bent and fondled its head.

"Bruno! Come here!" the farmer shouted.

From the sound of his voice he was somewhere near the farm-house.

"Go on, boy," Harry muttered and gave the dog a gentle shove.

The dog looked at him and then ran off around the barn.

"Nice work," Don said.

He had found a door leading into the barn and had pushed it open.

"Come on."

He stepped into darkness and Harry followed him. As soon as Harry shut the door, Don took out his flashlight from his pocket and swung the beam around.

"Up that ladder," he said.

They climbed the ladder and found themselves in a big loft, half-full of straw.

"This'll do us fine," Don said.

He crossed over to the loft door, pushed it open a few inches and peered down into the brick-stack.

Two men, one with a lantern, were just below him. They were listening.

"Could have been a cat, papa," the younger of the two said. "You know what Bruno is." He bent to fondle the dog who wagged his tail violently.

The farmer muttered to himself, then shrugging his shoulders, he turned back towards the house.

"Leave the dog loose," he said. "I'm not going to stay up all night just to please the police. What have they ever done for me?"

Both men re-entered the house and closed the door. Don heard the bolts slam home, and, after a few minutes, the light in the upstairs room went out.

"That was smart of you, Harry," he said going over to where Harry was already making himself comfortable in the straw. "They've turned in now."

Harry grinned.

"Wouldn't mind turning in myself, boss. Want anything to eat?"

"Not now. Let's get some sleep. We'll probably have to stay here all to-morrow and get moving again to-morrow night," Don said, relaxing back into the straw. "Once we get the other side of Padova, and into the hills we can risk moving in daylight."

Harry grunted.

"Anything you say, boss," he said sleepily.

A few moments later he was snoring gently.

Don lay awake, thinking. They were a long, long way from London. They had two frontiers to cross. He had no doubt of the difficulties. They were only on the first leg of their journey, and they were already being hunted by the police. He felt sure that Natzka wasn't remaining idle. He and his organization would be working frantically to block the way out of Italy, and if he and Harry did succeed in getting out of Italy, they still had to cross France.

It wasn't going to be easy. It was going to be a skilful game of fox and geese; one false move, and they would be trapped.

Don woke with a start to find Harry bending over him, gently shaking his arm.

Bright sunlight filtered through the cracks in the weather-shrunk timber of the barn. Don was immediately aware of sounds below, and he looked sharply at Harry.

"What's cooking?"

"There's a lorry just below us," Harry whispered. "It's going to Padova. They're loading it with vegetables now. Think we can steal a ride?"

Don got to his feet, hurriedly dusted himself down, then crossed to the door of the loft, pushed it open an inch or so and looked down into the brick-yard.

Immediately below him was a big, ten-ton truck, half covered with a sun-faded green tarpaulin. In the lorry, piled high, were crates of cabbages.

The elderly farmer and a young dark Italian who Don guessed was Vittore were talking to the lorry driver. As he watched, the three men moved off towards the farmhouse.

Don instantly made up his mind.

"Let's go, Harry."

They both put on their rucksacks and went back to the loft door. The lorry driver, the old farmer and Vittore had disappeared.

Don pushed open the door and dropped on to the crates of cabbages. Working quickly he shifted some of the crates to make enough room for himself and Harry to sit.

He looked up at Harry who was waiting.

"Okay."

Harry balanced himself on the ledge of the loft door, closed the door, hung by his fingers until he had adjusted his balance, then dropped into the space Don had cleared.

They sat down on the floor of the lorry and pulled the crates around them, forming a small square.

They had barely completed their task before they heard voices.

"See you to-morrow," the lorry driver called.

The old farmer wished him good journey, the lorry engine woke into life. The lorry jolted over the rough cart track to the main road.

Harry leaned his back against one of the crates and grinned at Don.

"If there's one thing I hate more than another it's eating cabbage, boss," he said. "But from now on, I'll live on the blessed stuff."

"Are we going right into Padova or shall we drop off before we get there?" Don said, frowning. He took out his map and began to study it while Harry, leaning over his shoulder, breathed heavily down his neck. "We'll drop off just outside Padova," Don went on after he had examined the map. "We'll make for Abano, which is in the hill district. From there we'll walk to Barbano, and on to the main road to Vicenza. We can pick up the C.I.T. bus to Brescia if we are lucky, and from Brescia, we are within striking distance of Milan."

"Always providing we don't run into a snag," Harry said.

"Yes." Don tried to make himself more comfortable as the lorry jolted and rattled over the uneven road. "Even if we get a break and reach Milan, we have still to get on a plane. Well, let's get to Milan before we worry about that. We can work out the difficulties when we come to them."

For half an hour, they sat side by side in the swaying, jolting lorry as it rattled along towards Padova, then Don began to check the terrain against the details of his map.

"We shouldn't be long now. In another ten minutes I reckon we should be in Padova."

Harry began to shift the crates so that they could drop off the tailboard of the lorry.

The country was still depressingly flat and exposed. In the far distance they could see peasants working in the fields.

"Once we leave this rattle-trap," Harry said, "we'll stick out like a neon light on a foggy night."

"We can't risk going straight into Padova. They'll be on the look-out for us." Don said, putting on his rucksack.

He pointed to the row of distant hills. "If we can reach those without trouble, we should be okay, but we've got to get to them first."

They were now sitting on the tailboard of the lorry, their legs hanging over the fast-moving road.

"Ready, boss?" Harry asked.

Don nodded.

They twisted over, hung for a moment and dropped off.

As soon as they had regained their balance, they ran over to the stone wall, skirting the road. There, they were out of sight of the distant peasants.

Harry lit a cigarette while he studied the land that lay ahead of them.

"Can't cross that lot without being seen," he said.

"How long do you think it'll take us to reach those hills?" Don asked.

"About an hour over this ground."

Don looked at his wrist watch. The time was twenty minutes past nine.

"Maybe we should have stayed in the barn, Harry. We're right out in the open now."

"There's no one in sight except those peasants," Harry returned, "and why should they bother about us? We've come thirty miles, and that's something. I think it's been worth the risk."

"Yes. Well, come on, let's go."

They climbed the wall and set off across the field. The going was heavy and their brisk speed was reduced. They kept looking across the field at the peasants working some five hundred yards or so away. None of them appeared to be looking in their direction. Some of them were digging sugar beet, others were lopping off the green heads of the beet with their big, curved knives, others were loading carts.

Don and Harry began to cross a wide stretch of undulating land of rough grass that led down into a sloping valley at the bottom of which were the first of the foothills, gradually leading to the big, brown and green hills that skirted the river Bacchiglione.

They were half-way across this stretch of grassland when faintly in the distance they heard a shout.

"That's done it!" Harry said, looking back over his shoulder.

Don looked back, too.

Against the skyline, three of the peasants were waving at them.

"Keep going," Don said, lengthening his stride. "Run if they do."

"What's their idea, boss?"

"They've either been tipped off by the police or they're Natzka's men," Don said. "If we can get them away from the others, we can tackle them easily enough."

Once again they looked back, then stopped short.

The three peasants had disappeared.

"Ah-uh," Don said. "Looks like they've gone to collect their pals. Feel like a little run, Harry?"

They broke into an easy, steady trot; a trot that they both knew they could keep up for some time, and that took them over the ground at a pretty fair pace.

"We've got to get to the hills before the police get here," Don said, breathing evenly.

He increased his pace, and together they ran down the sloping grassland to the distant hills.

They were both panting slightly as they climbed the stone wall at the bottom of the grassland, trotted across the rough road and climbed yet another stone wall.

They paused to look back.

Spread out on the skyline were six men; three of them by their hats were peasants; the other three were bareheaded and too far away for Don to see who they could be.

"Here they come," he said. "Come on; let's show them how to run!"

They set off at a fast pace. The going now was slightly uphill and it was a strain to keep up the pace, but they stuck to it, and it wasn't until they had breasted the slope that they again looked back.

The six men had broken formation. Some of them were still lumbering down the hill. Two had reached the stone wall and were clambering over it. Another was just beginning a staggering run up the slope, and even as they watched, he came to a halt while he struggled to get back his breath.

"Doesn't look as if they're in training, does it?" Harry grinned as Don swung around and began to run down the slope. They kept in step until they reached yet another stone wall; then Don came to an abrupt halt.

"The railway! I'd forgotten that."

They looked down into the steep cutting at the single line track.

"Our luck!" Harry said, cocking his head on one side. "There's a train coming now."

"Down we go," Don said, and together they scrambled down the steep bank on to the line.

There was a clump of shrubs not far down the line, and they ran, panting, towards it. They had barely reached it, and got behind it when the train came chugging along the track.

It was a long, heavily-laden goods train, and not moving more than fifteen miles an hour.

"It's a piece of cake," Harry said. "Soon as the engine's passed us, we nip out and get aboard."

At this moment the engine passed them. They could see the driver and the fireman in the cab. Then Harry caught hold of Don's arm and shoved him out from behind the shrub.

They waited on the track for the first wagons to pass, then when they spotted a low, open truck on which a brightly-painted farm tractor was tied, they dashed forward, ran alongside for a couple of breathless seconds, then swung on board.

"Under cover," Don gasped, and rolled under the tractor.

Harry followed him, and they kept flat while the train, slowly picking up speed, went rumbling and rattling through the cutting.

"They'll have guessed we're on board," Don said, after he was satisfied that they were out of sight of their pursuers. "They'll get to a telephone and warn the station ahead of us."

"They've got to reach a telephone first."

"Not if those guys were police. They'll have a car with a

transmitter on board." Don took out his map, studied it and put it back into his rucksack. "The next station up the line is Castelfranco. There's another railway line that crosses it at that station and goes to Vincenza. If we can pick up a train on that line without being seen we'll be doing well."

"Have we far to go on this lot?"

"About ten miles. It's better than walking." Don produced a packet of sandwiches Cherry had provided. "We'd better eat while we can."

"Blimey! I could work my way through an ox; tail, horns and the lot," Harry said, sighing. He began to munch a sandwich. "What'll we do when we get to Vincenza?"

"We'll keep clear of the centre of the town. We want more food, and we must find out if we can pick up a night bus to Verona. If things look sticky, we'll have to make for the hills again."

"Anything you say," Harry said, finishing his sandwich. "If we're going to restock our larder, how about another sandwich now?"

The big cream and blue C.I.T. bus pulled up under the single dim light above the bus stop. Two peasants in their Sunday best, a tired, shabby-looking commercial traveller with two heavy suitcases and a woman with a bundle done up in a gaudy shawl left the bus shelter and moved over to the bus.

There were only two passengers already in the bus, and both of them were women.

Don touched Harry's arm and nodded. They walked briskly from behind the bus shelter and got on board. Don bought tickets for Verona. Then they settled down two seats behind the driver.

The bus moved off, and Don and Harry exchanged relieved glances.

They had reached the outskirts of Vincenza soon after mid-day, and, having bought a small stock of food, they had spent the rest of the afternoon and evening in a small movie-house. No one had taken any notice of them, and when Don decided it must be dark enough to go out on the streets, they had checked the bus time-table and had found a bus was due to leave for Verona at nine-thirty.

"So far so good," Don muttered to Harry. "When we get to Verona we might see if we can steal a car. I don't think we have a hope of hiring one. If we can reach Brescia before day-light we really are making progress."

"You wouldn't take the car into Milan?" Harry asked.

Don shook his head.

"Before we get to Milan we have the autostrada to negotiate, and that's worrying me. We could avoid it, but it would mean going a long way out of our way."

"What's an autostrada, boss?"

"This particular one is the Milan-Brescia motor road with check points at either end. You have to buy a ticket to use the road, and there are always police guards."

"Best thing would be to jump a lorry, and hole up as we did last time."

"They'll be on the look-out for us. They may even be search-ing lorries."

"Maybe we'd better plan to take the longer way round."

"When we've got the car we can decide that."

It was a little after ten minutes past ten when the bus slowed down and pulled up outside the bus stop at Tavernelle.

Although both Don and Harry were alert for trouble, it came so quickly they were both momentarily caught on the wrong foot.

There was no light outside the bus stop, and looking through the window of the bus they could only see their own reflections from the light inside the bus.

The bus door jerked open and a crash helmetted motor-cycle cop blocked the doorway. He was a little man, his goggles up on his crash helmet, a carbine across the back of his shoulders, his right hand on the butt of an automatic in a holster at his waist.

His quick eyes swept over the passengers in the bus, then they concentrated on Don and Harry.

"That's torn it," Harry said out of the corner of his mouth without moving his lips.

The cop beckoned to them.

"Please step outside," he said curtly.

Don looked at him blankly.

"Speaking to me?" he said in English.

"Outside, signore," the cop said also in English.

"What's the idea?"

The other passengers in the bus were staring. The driver had swung around and was looking uneasily at the cop.

"I wish to see your papers," the cop went on to Don.

135

Don shrugged, got up, pulled his rucksack from the luggage rack and stepped into the gangway.

"Is this going to take long?" the bus driver asked. "I'm behind schedule now."

"Do not wait for these two. You can go on," the cop said.

The driver shrugged his shoulders and turned his back on the cop who stepped down from the bus and waited in the road.

"We may have to take this guy," Don murmured as he pretended to help Harry down with his rucksack. "Watch his gun hand."

They climbed down into the road and were a little startled to find two other motor-cycle cops, one of them with his carbine in his hand, waiting.

The bus driver slammed the door of the bus after them, engaged gear and drove away.

The first cop snapped on the headlights of his motor-cycle, lighting up the road.

"Your papers, please, signore," he said to Don.

As Don reached inside his windbreaker, he saw the second cop raise his carbine and point it at him. Don produced his passport and handed it to the cop.

The cop glanced at it, nodded and held out his hand for Harry's passport.

"Let him have it," Don said.

Harry handed the passport over.

"You are both under arrest," the cop said. "You will come with us."

"What's the charge?" Don asked mildly and he lifted his hat to scratch his head. It was a signal he had used before to warn Harry to be ready to start something.

Harry reacted immediately. He was holding his heavy rucksack over his shoulder. He gave a sudden heave, and, using the rucksack like a sling, he flung it into the face of the cop with the gun. At the bottom of the rucksack was a pair of nail-studded boots, and in spite of the leather and canvas covering of the rucksack the boots made a formidable weapon. The iron-bound heels caught the cop on the bridge of his nose, stunning him. He dropped the carbine and fell forward on hands and knees.

The other two cops went for their automatics, but stopped short as Don showed them the gun that had jumped into his hand.

"Don't move!" he rapped out.

Harry grabbed up the carbine and covered the fallen cop who was shaking his head and cursing.

"Turn around you two!" Don snapped.

The two cops turned round, and Don took away their automatics. He then unarmed the third cop who by now had got unsteadily to his feet.

Working swiftly, Harry removed a sparking plug from one of the motor-cycles, and pocketing it, he started up the other two cycles.

"Ready when you are, boss," he said.

Don unloaded the three automatics and threw the clips away, then he dropped the automatics in the road.

He went up to the first cop and dug him in the ribs with his gun.

"The passports!" he said.

Without turning round, the cop handed the passports to Don.

"Don't think you can get far," the cop said.

"At least we can try," Don said and grinned. "Walk down the road – the three of you. March!"

The three cops went away into the darkness.

Harry was already sitting astride one of the motor-cycles.

"Let's show these Eye-ties what speed really means," he said.

Don swung his leg over the other machine and he settled himself in the saddle.

"Let's go."

With the throttles wide open, they roared out of Tavernelle and along the main road to Verona.

# CHAPTER TWELVE

*Out of the Sky*

AFTER twenty minutes of fast riding during which time they had overtaken the C.I.T. bus and had long left it behind, Don signalled to Harry to reduce speed. He pulled in close to him, resting his hand on his shoulder so they could ride almost knee to knee.

"We'll have to get off the road soon. They'll be after us like a swarm of hornets now, and you can bet they've alerted all the mobile police in the district."

Harry pulled a face.

"I was enjoying this, boss. This bike can move."

"There's a road ahead on the right we'll take. It leads into the hills and it's a dead end. From there we'll have to walk again," Don said. "With any luck they'll think we've gone on to Verona."

"Okay," Harry said. "I'll be sorry to get off this bike; it's a beaut."

They again increased speed and before long, Don pointed ahead.

"There's the road; coming up now," he shouted.

They both cut down speed, swung round to their right and found themselves on a narrow, twisting road that climbed steeply.

Don went on ahead. They kept up a fifty mile an hour pace until the going got so rough and steep they had to cut down to a crawl.

It was a magnificent night with a high, full moon to light up the hills, and they turned off their headlamps as they could see clearly enough where they were going.

At the top of the hill, Don slowed and stopped. He sat astride the motor-cycle while he looked down the steep hill at the small village away in the distance.

"We're not all that far from the Swiss frontier from here, Harry. I think we might have a shot at getting into Switzerland rather than try for a plane in Milan. The Swiss police won't worry us, and we shouldn't have any trouble getting a plane from Zurich. As far as I can judge from the map, it'll take us about four days' hard walking to get to Tirano, the frontier town. From there we can get a car."

"Okay," Harry said. "How do we go?"

"Time to ditch these bikes. We can't ride past that village. They'll hear our engines and might report us. Let's get the bikes off the road and hidden."

It took them some minutes to find a thicket large enough in which to hide the motor-cycles. They laid them down, covered them with scrub until Don was satisfied they wouldn't be easily found.

"Okay; let's go," he said, and started off down the road.

They walked steadily for four hours; scarcely exchanging a word, keeping up the same swinging pace, climbing hills, scrambling down rocky inclines, by-passing sleeping villages, until suddenly Don called a halt.

"We can't be far from the main Trento road now," he said. "Should be over the next lot of hills unless I've made an error somewhere. Anyway, let's eat, have a drink and a smoke. We're doing fine."

They sat down on the hilltop and ate a hasty meal.

"Is that a lake over there, boss?" Harry asked, his mouth full.

"That's Lake Garda. We come out at the top end of it, then we have a long hike across the hills that are really small mountains. There are very few roads; mostly cart tracks. It'll be a rough trip, Harry."

Harry stretched his sturdy legs and grinned.

"I'm enjoying every bit of it up to now," he said. "At least, I'm seeing the country."

Don laughed.

"Am I glad I sent for you! This could be a pain in the neck alone." He got to his feet. "Well, come on; let's enjoy some more of it."

Sunlight was edging the distant mountain caps with a red rim as they reached and crossed the main Verona-Trento road, a few miles above the village of Ala. They once more began to climb, and by the time they reached the top of the first range of hills, the sun had swung up behind the mountains and the chill morning air began to warm up.

"I guess we'll bed down and have a sleep," Don said, flopping on the damp grass. "How's this for a view?"

From where they were they had a clear view of Lake Garda as it lay asleep in the sunlight. Around the lake were the mountains; between the hill they were on and the lake were meadows,

139

farmhouses and trees laid out like a child's toy on a drawing-room carpet.

"Terrific!" Harry exclaimed. He took a long pull from a bottle of Chianti they had bought, wiped his mouth with the back of his hand with a contented sigh and unrolled two ground-sheets he had taken from his rucksack. "Let's hit the hay."

They settled down, and after a while, they fell asleep. They slept for a couple of hours, and it might have been longer had not Don been woken by what sounded to him like the drone of a big bumble bee.

He frowned, opened his eyes, blinked up the dark blue sky. He listened lazily, then stiffening, he reached out and shook Harry's arm.

"Don't move!" he cautioned. "Listen!"

"Sounds like an aircraft . . ."

"It's a hover-plane. Look, there it is . . ."

Harry looked in the direction Don indicated.

Against the sunlight, scarcely visible, he could just make out the hover-plane, looking like a giant dragonfly several miles to their right.

"Can't be the police, boss?" Harry said.

Don shook his head.

"Might be Natzka's lot. Get under the ground-sheet. We won't take any chances. If it comes this way, just stay still. He can't spot us if we don't move."

The hover-plane flew on, passing them by several miles, then it turned back and flew in the opposite direction, this time a mile or so closer.

"I bet it's Natzka," Don said. "He's searching systematically. Two more journeys like that and he'll be right over us."

"Not much we can do, boss."

"No. He'll have a job to spot us. When he's on the most distant leg, crawl over to those shrubs. I'll go for those over there."

They waited until the hover-plane was once more only a distant speck, then moving quickly, they parted, and each lay out under the shrubs where they felt sure they couldn't be seen.

Ten minutes later the hover-plane returned. The sound of its engine was loud, and peering through the shrubs, Don could see how low it was now flying, skirting the tops of the hills with only twenty feet or so to spare. He suddenly wondered if they were all that safe, but it was too late to move now.

The hover-plane came on, flattening the rough grass with its slip-stream: a whirring, buzzing menace. It passed their hiding-place by a bare two hundred yards and flew on towards the lake.

"That was too close," Don said without moving from his hiding-place. "If he turns and comes back, he'll pass right over us."

"I've got something for him if he spots us," Harry called, and he waved his automatic. "At that range, he's going to get a surprise."

"Don't show yourself or shoot at him unless he starts something first," Don warned. "This may be nothing to do with Natzka."

"Okay," Harry said, "but I bet it is."

"We must wait, Harry . . ."

"I can't see what he can do, anyway."

"He can bring the others on to us by radio."

"They've got a long way to come if he does."

"Watch out! Here he comes!"

The hover-plane had turned annd was heading back towards them. The machine had slowed and was scarcely moving. As it came towards the hilltop, it dipped a little coming down once more to twenty feet.

Don felt naked and exposed. Could the pilot see him? He was obviously concentrating on this hill now. Looking up, Don saw the cabin door was open. He could see a man leaning out: a man with a dark, lean face – it was Curizo!

Don had scarcely time to register this fact when the hover-plane reached the exact spot where Harry and he were crouching.

The shrubs that concealed them swayed and parted under the impact of the slip-stream.

He had one brief glimpse of Curizo's face lighting up with a snarling smile; then something that looked like a cricket ball dropped from Curizo's hand and came hurtling down towards him.

"Look out!" he shouted. "It's a grenade!"

He heard the crack of Harry's automatic, then the grenade landed between the two shrubs in which he and Harry were hiding.

There was a flash and a bang. Don felt the earth heave a little, then something struck him on the side of his head, and the blue sky suddenly turned black.

"Boss! Boss! Are you all right?"

Harry, white-faced and anxious, was bending over him.

Don grunted, raised his hand to his aching head and opened his eyes.

For a moment Don couldn't remember what had happened, then he half sat up, grimacing, feeling blood running down his face.

"A stone must have caught me," he muttered.

"Don't move yet, boss."

"I'm all right."

"Let me fix that cut. It'll stop bleeding in a moment."

Don relaxed back while Harry found the first-aid pack from the rucksack and attended to the cut on his forehead.

"What happened?"

"The rat threw down the grenade, but I hit him in the arm," Harry said. "That put him out of action, and the kite steered off. It's down in the valley. You can see it from here. They'll be coming up on foot in a little while."

Don made an effort, sat up and then got unsteadily to his feet.

"That was close, Harry. We were lucky it was no worse."

"I thought you had had it. It gave me a nasty turn," Harry said, turned and pointed. "Look, there it is, by that farmhouse."

Don looked down the hill. Some ten miles away he could make out a small isolated farm house standing in lush green fields; near the farmhouse stood the hover-plane.

Harry was staring through a pair of powerful field glasses.

"They're getting Curizo out. There are five men and there's a girl . . ."

"Let's look, Harry."

Don took the glasses. The hover-plane suddenly jumped into his vision as if it were only a hundred yards or so from him as he looked through the eye-pieces of the glasses. He recognized Brun, Busso and Hans who were standing by the hover-plane. In the doorway of the farmhouse was Maria Natzka. She was wearing a white silk shirt and black slacks, and from her expression, she seemed amused by the excitement that was going on around the hover-plane.

He could see Carl Natzka talking to a short, thin man who was holding a flying helmet and who Don guessed was the pilot.

Curizo was lying on the grass, and no one seemed to be paying him any attention.

The pilot turned and pointed directly at the hilltop where Don was standing.

Natzka appeared to shout, for the three men grouped around the hover-plane turned and went to him. He pointed to the hilltop. There was a moment's talk, then they ran over to a big outbuilding. The double doors were opened and a car drove out, followed by another car. Four more men appeared and got into the first car. Busso, Hans and Brun got into the second car. The two cars drove down the cart-track on to the road, and then, with increasing speed, they drove rapidly towards Don's hilltop.

"Here they come," he said, slipping the glasses into the leather case. "It'll take them the best part of two hours to get here, Harry. Our move is to get off this hill and get around the back of it. If we could get to that hover-plane, I could handle it."

Harry's face brightened.

"That's an idea, boss. But do you feel like a dash down there?"

"I'll have to feel like it. It's our best bet."

For all that, Don still felt dazed and unsteady, and he was glad to have Harry's help as they went down the hill.

It took them a long ten minutes to get off the hill. Then began the cautious move around the hill into the rocky, shrub-covered ground that lay between them and the distant farmhouse.

Don had calculated it was a good seven miles to the farmhouse from where they were, and with a badly aching head and legs that felt weak and unsteady, he realized it was going to be a tough journey.

The rising road hid them from the distant road, and they slogged on for the next hour, plodding over the rough ground, alert and tense.

They had covered about four miles when the ground suddenly began to slope, and at the ridge of the hill, they paused, went down on hands and knees and looked below.

They could see the two cars now parked by the roadside. Busso had been left to guard the cars while the other men were moving towards the hill.

Don studied the terrain.

"Not much cover down there, Harry," he said. "We'll have to put those two cars out of action before we can make for the farmhouse, and we'll have to take care of the guard."

Harry watched the seven men as they climbed slowly towards them. He judged where they would reach the ridge and decided

143

they would be about fifty yards or so from where Don and he lay hidden in the scrub.

"We'll have to let them get to the foot of the hill before we can tackle fatso down there," he muttered in Don's ear. "They won't be able to see him from there."

Don nodded and crouched lower as Brun pulled himself over the ridge.

"I don't see why we should all climb that hill," Brun grumbled as another tall, heavily-built man joined him on the ridge. His voice came clearly to Don and Harry. "Curizo said they were both dead. He dropped the grenade right on top of them. Why can't the others go up and we stay here?"

"Busso said they might not be dead. Come on; and shut up!" the other man growled, and panting heavily, he continued his slow climb towards the hill.

Grumbling, Brun went after him.

Some twenty minutes crawled by before the seven men began to descend the slope that led to the foot of the hill. As soon as they were out of sight, Don and Harry, crouching low, slid over the ridge and made for the road.

They could see Busso sitting on the bank, his back to them, smoking a cigarette.

"I'll take him, boss," Harry muttered. "You stay behind the bush down there. When I'm ready I'll raise my hand. I'll have to rush him for the last few yards. May be if you threw a stone, you'd distract his attention."

Don nodded. That made sense. He was still feeling groggy, and he knew Harry was much more capable in a rough house than he was.

"As soon as you reach him, I'll come down."

Harry grinned.

"I won't need any help. You fix the cars, boss."

Again Don nodded.

They continued down the slope until they reached the bush Harry had indicated.

Busso had got to his feet and was wandering up and down the road. From time to time he looked up towards the hill, scowling. Looking back, Don could see the seven men half-way up the hill; they were taking it very slowly, and he could hear Busso cursing them. Then, shrugging his fat shoulders, Busso went back to the bank and sat down again.

Harry nudged Don.

"Here I go," he whispered, slipped off his rucksack and began to crawl quickly down the bank, keeping the odd shrubs that dotted the bank between himself and Busso.

Don watched him, marvelling at Harry's speed and silence. Harry paused behind the last scrap of cover. Busso's broad back was within ten yards of him. He looked back over his shoulder at Don and raised his hand.

Don had already located a big flint stone. He half rose and threw the stone with all his strength at Busso's head.

The stone whizzed through the air, and Busso, hearing it, half started up. The stone caught him between the shoulders. He gave a startled grunt and staggered forward.

Harry was up and moving while the stone was in mid-air. He jumped the remaining yards, dropped on Busso, bringing him sprawling into the dust.

Don saw Harry's fist rise and fall, then Busso went limp.

Harry stood up and grinned.

"Nothing to it, boss," he said and ran over to one of the cars, lifted the bonnet and removed the distributor head.

Don caught up Harry's rucksack and came tumbling down into the road.

"We'll take the other car, Harry." He bent and snatched up Busso's big black hat. "Come on; get in!"

He put on the hat, slid under the driving-wheel and started the engine. Harry opened the off-side door and got in.

Very far away there came a faint shout, and Harry looked back up the hill.

Two of the men who had reached the top of the hill were waving to the others who were not high up enough to see the road.

"They've spotted us," Harry said as Don made a U-turn and sent the car shooting down the road towards the farm-house.

"They haven't a hope of catching us," Don said. "Keep out of sight, Harry. With any luck they'll think I'm Busso come back to report."

"Good show!" Harry said and sat down on the floorboards.

Don drove swiftly down the road. It was a three to four mile stretch to the farmhouse, and he reckoned it would take the men well over an hour, even if they ran most of the way, to get off the hill and get back to the farmhouse. He had that much in hand to put Natzka, the pilot and Maria out of action and get the hover-plane going. It would be nip and tuck, he thought grimly, but it could be done.

"Running through the farm gates in another minute," he said to Harry and braked sharply. He slid down in the driver's seat, jerked the big hat lower over his face and swung through the white gateposts.

The car bumped over the uneven road. Not far off stood the hover-plane. There was no one in it nor by it. Don was tempted to stop the car and make a dash for it, but he knew he had to immobilize those left in the house first.

Harry had taken out his automatic and rested it on his knee. His hand lay on the car door-handle, ready to press it down and jump out.

"No one about," Don muttered, and one hand on the steering-wheel and his right hand holding his automatic out of sight, he pulled up outside the farmhouse door.

Don had hoped that Natzka might have come to the door and he could have surprised him, but he quickly realized that he would have to make the first move.

"You keep out of sight, Harry," he said softly. "I'll tackle this. If I put my foot wrong, you'll be there to pull me out."

"Let me go, boss," Harry said urgently.

"No; do what I tell you!"

Don opened the car door, crossed the patch of garden in three long strides, turned the handle of the front door and pushed.

The door swung inwards.

Don found himself looking into a small hall. Facing him was a flight of steep stairs. There was a door on his left which he assumed led into the main room.

He hadn't time to have more than one fleeting glimpse of the hall for he saw the pilot of the hover-plane coming down the stairs.

The pilot stopped short, his mouth opening, his eyes popping.

"Make a sound and I'll blow your head off!" Don said softly showing his gun.

The pilot raised his hands above his head, his face draining white.

"Come down," Don said.

Slowly, as if he were walking on egg-shells, the pilot descended the stairs until he was within a few feet of Don.

"Turn around!"

Reluctantly the man turned his back on Don who ran his

hand over him. When he found he wasn't carrying a gun, he stepped back.

"Where are the others?"

The pilot indicated a door at the end of the passage.

"Go ahead, and don't try any tricks."

The pilot walked down the passage, turned the handle of the door and entered a big roughly-furnished room.

Don stepped quickly up to him and gave him a violent shove that sent him flying into the room to land on hands and knees near where Carl Natzka was sitting.

"Don't move!" Don rapped out.

"Why, if it isn't Mr. Micklem," Maria said.

She was seated by the window, knitting with scarlet and white wool. She smiled at him, her knitting needles continuing to fly, her eyes bright with excitement.

Natzka had been studying a large scale map which was spread over his knees. At the sight of Don, his face paled and his mouth tightened. The map slid off his knees on to the floor.

"How nice," Maria went on. "I've been so worried about you. What's happened to your head?"

"One of your brother's pals threw a grenade at me," Don said. "But like all your brother's pals he was very inefficient, and he didn't do a great deal of damage."

"Oh, darling," Maria said, looking reproachfully at Natzka, "must you have grenades thrown at Mr. Micklem? After all, he is a friend of mine."

"Be quiet!" Natzka said harshly. "I want to talk to you," he went on to Don. "You can't get out of the country. Every road is watched; the police are looking for you. There are special guards at all the frontier towns. Sooner or later you must be caught. I'll do a deal with you ..."

"I'm not interested in any deal with you," Don said curtly.

Where was Curizo? he was wondering and he moved sideways so his back wasn't towards the door.

"I want that book, Micklem," Natzka said. "I'll buy it from you ..."

"Really, Carl, that's absurd," Maria broke in. "Mr. Micklem is a millionaire ..."

"You're not having the book, so save your breath," Don said.

"You okay, boss?" Harry called from down the passage.

"Yes. Curizo's somewhere in the house. Find him and put him out of action, then come back here and hurry," Don said without taking his eyes off Natzka.

The pilot remained on the floor. He stared uneasily at Don, and then looked at Natzka.

"Are you going to put us out of action, too, Mr. Micklem?" Maria asked. "How will you do that: knock us on the head?"

She was laughing at him.

"A length of rope is all that's necessary," Don said, smiling. "Your brother's pals will be back to release you in a little while."

"I am so relieved. I was frightened you were going to be as brutal as my brother," she said. "I do apologize for Carl's behaviour. The trouble with him is he values life so very highly. If he doesn't get that silly little book back, he will be put against a wall and shot." She paused in her knitting to study the pattern, then the needles began to fly again. "And so shall I. Carl doesn't want to be killed. Of course, I don't either, but I don't approve of killing and hurting people just to save my own skin."

"Your sentiments do you credit, but they didn't stop your brother murdering John Tregarth," Don said quietly. "The situation isn't perhaps so dramatic as you make it appear. You need not return and admit failure. You can drop out of sight."

She laughed, and again he thought he had never seen a woman as beautiful as she.

"Where would we hide? They are patient and powerful. They don't forget. They would find us sooner or later as I am afraid they will find you, Don. I am quite sure you are very brave and your nerves are very steady, but I do assure you that if you don't give up the book, sooner or later you will lose your life. It may take months, but one day you will meet with an accident – one of our famous engineered accidents. You can't escape it."

"What am I supposed to do?" Don said, smiling. "Break down and cry?"

She shook her head.

"I just happen to like you. I'd hate to think of you dead."

"But since, according to you, you will be dead a long time before they catch up with me, I don't see why you should be so anxious," Don returned. "Sorry, but I'm not influenced by your argument."

"I can but warn you, Don."

Harry came in at this moment, carrying a coil of rope.

"I found Curizo upstairs," he said. "He didn't make any trouble."

"Rope this guy," Don said, pointing to the pilot.

"You can't get away," Natzka said. "I'll give you your life in return for the book. I must have the book!"

"Don't talk through the back of your neck!" Don said. "Of course we can get away. We're using the hover-plane."

Natzka's face went chalk white.

"You can't handle it!"

"You forget, Carl, that Mr. Micklem is an expert pilot," Maria said, and in spite of her smile, her face paled too. "I don't think you have been very clever to give him such an easy opportunity to get away."

"Be quiet!" Natzka exclaimed.

Harry completed roping the pilot, then crossed over to Natzka who suddenly jumped from his chair and caught at Harry's throat.

It was a move Harry had been expecting. He swept Nazka's hands away with his left arm and then slammed a right-hand punch to Natzka's jaw.

Natzka's eyes rolled back, he sagged at the knees and Harry shoved him back into the chair.

Maria caught her breath sharply as Harry hit her brother, and she turned away her head. Then she stiffened and looked out of the window.

"I should hurry, Don," she said. "They're coming down the road."

Harry jumped to the window.

"They are, boss! They must have picked up a car on the road."

He stepped behind Maria, dropped a loop of rope around her and fastened the rope to the back of the chair.

"I hope that's not too tight, miss," he said.

Harry was always courteous to the ladies.

She looked over her shoulder and gave him a dazzling smile.

"Don't worry about me." She looked at Don. "Goodbye. I hope you get away."

Don hesitated. He wondered if he should take her with him, then he remembered how she had nearly tricked him into leaving Venice. It was too risky. He couldn't trust her.

"Goodbye and good luck," he said.

"Let's go," Harry said, and together they ran out of the room.

As they reached and climbed into the hover-plane, they could see an open car with five men in it, speeding along the dusty road.

Don checked over the instrument panel, fired the starting cartridge and the overhead airscrew began to revolve.

Harry knelt at the open cabin door. As the car turned into the farm gateway, he raised his automatic and fired. The windshield of the car smashed and the car skidded to a standstill.

The five men jumped out and scattered.

Harry felt the hover-plane lift.

Busso, crouching behind the car, began to fire at the machine as it rose slowly in the air. A bullet zipped past Harry's face; another smashed the clock on the panel. Harry sent a bullet so close to Busso that he ducked back under cover.

All the men were shooting now and the air hummed with bullets, but the hover-plane was climbing and moving away.

"We've licked them," Don said as he pushed forward the throttles, and the hover-plane, gathering speed, climbed over the hills and out of range of the shooting.

# CHAPTER THIRTEEN

## Check

HARRY settled himself in the seat beside Don, reached for the rucksack at his feet and opened it.

"Phew! Now for a little relaxation," he said. He began to unpack a lump of salami sausage. He opened his pocket-knife and cut off a generous slice. "Can you eat while you handle this kite, boss?"

"I can always eat," Don said, and accepted the salami. "Don't scoff the lot, Harry, we may still need some."

"Aren't we going to London in this crate?"

"Not a hope. We haven't enough gas in her to last us twenty minutes."

"Blimey! Don't tell me we're going to start walking again," Harry said, his face alarmed.

Don nodded.

"I guess we are. We'll be lucky if we get across the frontier."

"Oh well, at least we've given his nibs the slip," Harry said reflectively. He chewed for some moments as he stared down at the mountain range that was looming towards them. "Where are you heading for, boss?"

"We've got to get across the frontier, Harry. We know they are on the look-out for us there. Once we're in Switzerland, we can take a train to Zurich and fly to London. Right now, we're heading for Tirano which is the frontier town. When we spot that, we go a few points north, and if we're lucky, we'll get to St. Moritz. It'll be a toss-up whether the gas holds out that long."

"Don't leave it too long," Harry said. "I wouldn't like to crash in this kite. It doesn't feel very substantial."

Don grinned.

"It isn't. It'd be quite a bump."

He glanced again at the petrol gauge. The indicator kept flicking over to zero. They were nearly dry; another three or four minutes would empty the tank completely.

"Any parachutes around, Harry?"

"Bad as that?" Harry said, his eyes popping a trifle. He looked hurriedly around. "Don't see any."

151

"Look! There's Tirano now," Don said.

Harry was looking behind the seats. He glanced over his shoulder at the small town below, then renewed his search.

"I've got them, boss. They don't look as if they've been checked in years."

"Dope that I am!" Don said angrily. "Of course! There's a reserve gas tank on board. If it's full, we'll just about get over that mountain range." A quick manipulation of switches brought a more welcome reading on the petrol gauge, and Don began to climb. "We're safe for about another twenty minutes. Get your map out, Harry."

Breathing heavily, Harry produced the map.

"We've got to find a spot where we can land. Look at these mountains!"

"I'm looking at them," Harry said uneasily. "Mind you don't knock them about, boss; they might knock back."

Scarcely fifty feet below them were the rocky, snow-covered mountain caps, guarding the Swiss frontier, and Don climbed higher.

"Well, come on; we're wasting time. How far is it from the plain?"

"Too far from the look of it, but I wouldn't know, boss."

"Let me have a look." Don studied the map, grunted and handed it back to Harry. "We'll just about do it if we have any luck."

"That's nice," Harry said, staring down at the snow-covered mountain. "Fancy landing in that stuff!"

Some ten minutes later, with the petrol gauge registering zero, they swam out of thick cloud and saw below them the flat, grazing pasture land dotted with goats, and in the distance the wooden houses of the peasants, sheltering at the foot of the mountains.

"We've done it!" Don said and put down the nose of the hover-plane.

A minute or so later he had made a perfect three-point landing a quarter of a mile from a secondary motor road that they could see winding up into the mountains.

"Let's get out of here before anyone comes to ask us what we're playing at," Don said, slipping on his rucksack.

"More walking now, boss?" Harry said, regretfully leaving the hover-plane.

"Unless we thumb a ride to St. Moritz."

They set off across the grass towards the road, and a few

minutes' quick walking brought them on to the road.

They looked back.

The hover-plane stood out against the mountain background far too conspicuously for their sense of comfort.

They walked briskly along the road, and they had covered a mile or so before they heard a distant motor-engine.

"We'll try for a lift," Don said, "but watch out. Have your gun handy."

"I'll watch it," Harry said.

A big lorry came down the road and Don waved. The lorry slowed down, and the driver, a good-natured looking man with keen blue eyes, gave them a friendly grin.

"Can you give us a lift to St. Moritz?" Don asked in his impeccable French.

"Jump in," the driver said. "I like company," and he opened the door of his cab.

Harry and Don scrambled in, slammed the door and the driver sent the lorry forward again.

During the ride, the lorry driver could talk of nothing but the hover-plane he had seen crossing the mountains.

Dressed as they were in their windbreakers and corduroy trousers, he took Don and Harry for ordinary hikers, and it didn't cross his mind that they had anything to do with the hover-plane. He was still wagging his head, and saying what an extraordinary thing it was, when they left him in the main street of the town.

"We'll go straight to the station and get a train for Zurich," Don said. "From there we can get a plane to London."

At the station they learned they had just missed a train, and there wouldn't be another for an hour.

"How about going to a restaurant, boss, and having a damn good blow-out?" Harry asked hopefully.

Don shook his head.

"We can't afford to waste a second. You can bet Natzka is organizing something for us. I'll see if I can hire a car. You go and buy some food, and meet me here in twenty minutes."

Harry's face fell.

"Anything you say, boss."

Fortunately, Don had spent several winter months at St. Moritz, and the manager of the Palace Hotel knew him well. Don arranged with a garage for the hire of a car, and in less than half an hour, he was driving down the main street towards the station in a powerful, black Bugatti.

Harry who was waiting for him, silently munching a hunk of sausage, grinned happily when he saw the car.

Before the war Harry had been number one mechanic to an international motor-racing star, and he lived and dreamed big cars.

"Phew! You've got something there, boss," he said. "Did you have to pinch it?"

"I got it from the hotel," Don said, sliding into the passenger's seat. Although he was a first-class driver himself, he knew Harry had the edge on him when it came to driving at speed. "Take her, Harry, and let's go."

Harry gulped down the last of the sausage, wiped his greasy fingers on the back of his trousers and got in under the steering wheel.

"I've got a sausage for you if you want it," he said, dumping his rucksack in the boot behind him.

"Not yet," Don said, busily examining his map. "We've about a hundred and fifty miles to go to Zurich on a good road." He looked at his wrist watch. The time was twenty minutes to four. "Allowing for traffic and the hair-pin bends, we should be there by about half-past eight."

"I'll do it faster than that, boss," Harry said, engaging gear and driving the car slowly down the main street. "This beauty can go."

"We can't afford to take any risks," Don said. "So watch out for accidents, Harry."

"How about petrol?"

"The tank's full, and I've got four two-gallon cans in the boot. We'll have more than we want."

"Okay," Harry said, and slightly increased his speed as the traffic ahead thinned.

But it wasn't until he got clear of the town and on to the Silvaplana road that he showed what he could get out of the big Bugatti. They reached Silvaplana in just under ten minutes, swung to the right and went storming up the mountain road towards Chur.

The road, carved out of the mountain side, twisted and turned like the back of a coiled snake, and in spite of the traffic coming down into Silvaplana, Harry kept up an average speed of forty-five miles an hour.

He had an uncanny talent of anticipation. It was as if he had a radar screen inside his head which warned him whether or not some lorry or car was coming from around the hidden bend.

Don noticed he automatically slowed down on some bends, and sure enough a car would appear, more often than not in the middle of the road, whereas on other bends, Harry ripped around them to find a clear road.

"We'll have to watch our step at the airport," Don said, once he was satisfied that Harry's mind could cope with conversation at the same time as he was concentrating on his driving. "Once we get on a plane to London, Natzka is beaten, and he must know it. He'll stage his last trick at the airport. Our best plan is for you to drop me off outside the airport, go in and get two tickets. They don't know you as well as they know me. I'll join you at the last moment on the plane."

"Wouldn't it be better if I dropped off and you stayed with the car, boss?" Harry said. "If I run into trouble, you can hop it in the car."

Don nodded.

"Sure, that's right. We'll do that. We may not run into trouble, of course. Natzka may think we're making for Milan. But we've got to be on the look-out. It's his life or ours."

"We'll watch out," Harry said, and settling himself further down in the bucket seat he gave himself up to his driving.

Forty minutes later, ten minutes better than Don had hoped was possible, Harry was slowing down to pass through Chur.

Once clear of the town, he again pushed down the accelerator, and the big car surged forward along the mountain-flanked road towards Sargans.

They were ten miles out of Chur, when Harry suddenly swore softly under his breath, and Don felt the speed of the car sharply fall off.

"What's up?" he asked.

"Can't be out of gas," Harry said, looking at the petrol gauge as the car slid slowly to a standstill.

"Of course we can't. I shoved in fifteen gallons at St. Moritz."

Harry opened the car door and got out.

"Maybe it's a choked feed," he said as he lifted the bonnet.

Don reached in the boot and found the tool kit. He joined Harry in the road.

Harry had been trained to trace faults quickly. It didn't take him more than a few minutes to find the trouble.

"Someone's put water in the petrol, boss."

"I certainly was kidding myself when I said Natzka's last trick would be tried at the airport," Don said. "Well, okay, let's get rid of it. Every minute we stay here gives him the chance of catching up with us."

"I'll drain out the tank and we'll fill up again. That's the quickest way."

Don went to the boot and lugged out the four petrol cans while Harry let the watered petrol run into the road.

It took a few minutes to empty the tank, then Don unscrewed the cap on one of the cans, took an experimental sniff at the can, and his mouth tightened to a hard line.

"This isn't gas, Harry," he said. "It's water!"

"Properly done it on us, haven't they?" Harry said, his face expressionless. "Well, we'll have to do something about it, won't we?" He began to strip down the carburettor. "We'll have to get some more. Maybe we could get a lift back to Chur."

"What a dope I've been!" Don said savagely. "I should have checked the gas. Tregarth warned me what we were up against. We won't give up the car, Harry. It'll be quicker to go back to Chur and get more petrol than thumb a ride in a car or a lorry."

"There was a garage just outside Chur," Harry said as he carefully cleaned the carburettor filters with his handkerchief. "I spotted it as we came out. A small place on the left-hand side."

Don began to empty the water out of the petrol cans.

"I'll go; you stick with the car. With any luck, I'll get a lift. You wait for me, Harry."

"I'll have everything checked and ready by the time you get back, boss."

Taking two cans in either hand, Don set off down the road, covering the ground with long, swinging strides.

He walked about half a mile before he heard a car coming. He set down the cans, shifted his automatic from his hip-pocket to the side-pocket of his windbreaker and kept his hand on the butt.

He was now much more conscious of Natzka's long, powerful arm than he had been, and he was determined to take no risks.

A small car came into sight, and, stepping into the middle of the road, Don waved.

The driver seemed reluctant to stop, but Don gave him no

alternative. If he had gone on, he would have run Don down.

The driver was a fat, elderly man; probably a commercial traveller, Don thought, and he stepped up to the driving window, his finger around the trigger of his hidden gun.

"Will you take me to Chur? I've run out of petrol," he said.

The fat man shrugged and opened the car door with bad grace.

"I'm not supposed to carry passengers," he grumbled, and scowled still more when Don put the petrol cans on the floor at the back of the driving seat.

He didn't speak the whole way to Chur, and when he dropped Don outside the small garage Harry had noticed, he drove off before Don could thank him.

A lanky man in overalls came out of a wooden hut beside a row of petrol pumps and looked hard at Don as Don set down the cans.

Don was instantly suspicious of this man. There was a furtive, uneasy expression in the small ferret-like eyes that warned Don to be alert.

"Fill these with your best petrol," he said, indicating the cans.

"You're too late. We're shut," the man growled and, turning, he went back into his hut.

It was a good half-mile further on to the main street of Chur, and Don wasn't wasting that much time.

He followed the lanky man into the hut. He entered the dim little room cautiously, and it was as well he did. Out of the corner of his eye he caught sight of the lanky man pressed up against the wall, his hand raised, and in his hand was a heavy wrench. He slammed a vicious blow at Don's head, but Don side-stepped, jumped into the room, jerking out his automatic as he did so.

"Watch it!" he said sharply.

The sight of the gun made the lanky man's eyes pop. He hurriedly dropped the wrench, his foxy face turning white.

"Okay," Don said, "you've had your fun, now get out there and fill those cans. I'm staying here, but don't think I can't put a slug in your leg from that range, because I can."

With knees that wobbled, the lanky man went out and began to fill the cans.

When they were filled, Don slipped the gun into his windbreaker pocket and kept his hand on the butt. He came out of the hut.

"Put the cans in that truck," he said, pointing to a break-down van that stood on a ramp near the pump. "Snap it up!"

The lanky man did as he was told.

"Get in," Don said. "You're going for a little ride."

Sullenly, the man got into the van and Don sat beside him.

"Make for the Sargans' road," Don said, "and get some speed into it."

When they were out of sight of the garage, Don said, "Did you get orders not to sell me gas?"

The lanky man didn't say anything.

Don dug him in the side with the gun.

"If you want to come out of this alive, you'd better talk," he snapped.

"They telephoned me," the lanky man snarled. "I was only obeying orders."

"You're a mug, but that's your funeral," Don said. "When did they telephone you?"

"About an hour back."

This information startled Don. It meant there must be a trap waiting for them by this time at the Zurich airport. Natzka was obviously covering every possible line of escape. This must also mean there would be a deputation waiting for them at the French-Swiss and the German-Swiss frontiers.

He was still considering the best way to beat Natzka when he saw ahead Harry waiting by the Bugatti.

"Stop by that car," Don told the lanky man.

When the van stopped, Harry ran up and unloaded the petrol cans. He started filling the Bugatti's tank while Don gave the lanky man enough money to cover the cost of the petrol.

"Now get back and keep your mouth shut," he said to him.

The lanky man glowered, reversed his van and drove away.

By the time Don reached the Bugatti, Harry was screwing on the cap to the tank.

"All ready, boss."

"We've lost an hour, but it can't be helped," Don said, getting in beside Harry. "Let her rip."

Once more they continued the journey, and Harry drove a shade faster, taking more risks, and he scarcely cut down speed as they went through Sargans and stormed on towards Wallenstadt.

Don told him what the lanky man had said about receiving orders on the telephone.

"Natzka must be sure we are heading this way, and you can

158

bet your last buck, he'll do everything he can to stop us getting on a plane."

"Should we stick to the car, boss?"

Don shook his head.

"We'd never get through the frontier post. The sooner we get rid of the car the safer it will be. That garage guy is certain to give a description of it, and they may try to fix us on the road. You get on with the driving. I'll try and figure something out."

Harry nodded and thumbed down the horn button, blasting the car ahead of him to one side so he could pass.

They were now running along the Zurich lake. Harry was too busy driving to appreciate the beauty of the scene. He was driving at just under ninety-five miles an hour, and it was all he could do to keep the great car steady on the uneven road.

Don said abruptly, "There's only one way out for us, Harry. We'll have to hole up somewhere until it gets dark, then we'll have to sneak into the airport and either pinch a plane or smuggle ourselves on board one."

"Blimey!" Harry said, startled. "That's not going to be easy."

"I'm hanged if I can think of any other way. They're certain to be waiting for us at the airport, and we must fly to get through the frontier posts."

Harry brooded for a moment, then grinned.

"How about you and me becoming stewards, boss?"

Don's face lit up.

"That could be an idea. Our first move is to get rid of the car as soon as we are within striking distance of the airport. We've got to get hold of a change of clothes and get into the airport. From there we must grab what chances are offered us, but kidnapping a couple of stewards and taking their places might be a good idea."

It was a minute after eight-forty-five when the Bugatti slackened speed and entered Zurich, and, considering they had lost an hour on the road, Don considered it a miraculous piece of driving on Harry's part.

They drove straight to the Europa Hotel where the manager of the Palace Hotel at St. Mortiz had asked Don to leave the Bugatti.

Taking Harry with him, Don interviewed the manager of the hotel, an elderly suave-looking man, who could have been a French diplomat.

At first he was a little frosty when he saw their dusty, travel-worn clothes, but when Don mentioned his name, he immediately thawed.

"Why, Mr. Micklem, of course. I recognize you now. Please come into my office. I am delighted to be of service to you. Did you wish for rooms?"

They followed him into his private office, then when Harry had closed the door, Don said, "We would like a room with a bath for a couple of hours. We also want a hot meal served in the room. Can you do that for us?"

"Certainly, Mr. Micklem; it will be a pleasure."

"We also want two outfits from two of your staff. Ordinary working suits, white shirts, ties and hats. I'm sorry I can't explain why we want them, but our need is urgent, and we will, of course, pay for them. Can you fix that for us too?"

The manager's face remained impassive, but not without an effort of will. He had been asked in the past for many odd things by his clients, but this request seemed to him to be the oddest.

"That can be arranged, Mr. Micklem," he said manfully.

"If anyone should ask for me or want to speak to me on the telephone, please tell them that I'm not here," Don went on.

The manager lifted his shoulders despairingly.

"Yes, certainly."

"Now, may we go to our room? If you could take us there yourself . . . in case one of your staff recognizes me."

The manager got up.

"Certainly, Mr. Micklem."

Half an hour later, bathed, shaved and freshened, wearing neat black suits that fitted fairly well, white shirts and black ties, Don and Harry sat down to a chicken *vol au vent* dinner, washed down by a bottle of the hotel's best wine.

As they were finishing the meal, the telephone bell rang. Don got up and lifted the receiver.

"This is the manager," and Don recognized the manager's voice. "A man has just been in to inquire for you. My clerk obeyed your instructions. He said you were not staying with us."

"Fine," Don said. "Did he get a description of the man?"

"He tells me he was short, powerfully-built and apparently an Italian."

"Thank you. Now, I would like to settle my account. We shall be leaving very shortly."

"Certainly. I will come up myself."

Don replaced the receiver and looked at Harry.

"They are right on our heels. Busso has been asking for us."

Harry grinned cheerfully.

"Well, they haven't caught us yet, boss."

"No, but we mustn't underestimate Natzka," Don said seriously. "He must be certain now that we are somewhere in Zurich. Everything depends for him on whether we slip through his fingers or not. This is going to be tough, and make no mistake about it." He lit a cigarette and began to pace up and down.

"When should we go?" Harry asked.

"There's a plane out for London at eleven o'clock. We have just under two hours," Don returned. "I'm trying to think what I would do in Natzka's place. Obviously, I would have the airport guarded. We may find, Harry, that we won't be able to get near the airport. If we are lucky and do get near it, we may not be able to get near a plane." While he was talking, he stood before the mantelpiece that was strewn with attractive little nicknacks. He picked up a small, square-shaped box and turned it over in his fingers. Then he smiled. "I'm going to lay a false trail, Harry."

Harry looked interested.

"How are you going to do that?"

Don took off his coat, opened his shirt and removed the body-belt around his waist. He took from the belt the leather-bound book that Tregarth had entrusted to him. He carried the box he had found on the mantelpiece and the oilskin-packed book to the table and sat down.

"Stand by the door, Harry."

Harry obeyed. He watched Don unpack the book and put it in his pocket. He then wrapped the box in the oilskin covering and sealed it as carefully as it had been originally sealed.

"Right," he said. "The next move is to get to the American consul here, and that's not going to be easy."

"The consul?" Harry said, looking puzzled. "What's the idea?"

A tap sounded on the door. Don whipped the oilskin package out of sight, crossed the room and stepped into the bathroom, gun in hand.

"See who it is," he said quietly.

Cautiously Harry opened the door, found the hotel manager outside, and let him in.

Don put away his gun and came into the room again.

"I have your account, Mr. Micklem," the manager said. "Is there anything else we can do for you?"

"You can tell me where I can find the American consulate," Don said, taking the account.

"Certainly; it is merely a few buildings down the road. You leave the hotel, turn left and you will see the flag above the building."

"Thank you." Don settled the account. "And thank you for making our short stay such a comfortable one. Is there a back way out we could use?"

Again the manager had to make an effort not to show his surprise. This wealthy young American, he thought, was behaving in an extraordinary manner; almost as if he were a criminal.

"At the end of the corridor, you will find a service lift. That will take you down to the back exit."

"Fine. Well, thanks again. We'll be leaving almost at once."

When the manager had bowed himself out, Don sat down at the writing desk, scribbled a note, put it in an envelope and sealed it with sealing wax.

"I guess we can go," he said to Harry. "Leave the rucksacks here. With any luck we shan't be needing them again."

"I still don't know what it's all about," Harry said plaintively. "Why do we go to the consul?"

"I'll tell you as we go down," Don said, opened the door, peered up and down the deserted corridor, then nodded. "All clear. Let's go."

As the service lift carried them down to the ground floor, Don briefly outlined his scheme.

"Whatever happens I must give the book to Sir Robert Graham myself. Tregarth warned me to trust no one, and I don't intend to. Natzka doesn't know this. I am going to ask the consul to deliver the oilskin package containing the box and not the book to the London ambassador. He'll fly it in the diplomatic bag, and I'm hoping Natzka will guess this is what I'll attempt to do. If he has someone working at the consulate, and I bet he has, the news will leak out that I have given the package to the consul. I'm hoping once he knows I haven't the book, he'll leave us alone. After all, it's not us he wants; it's the package. If I fool him, we should be able to board a plane without difficulty."

Harry nodded.

"That's right, boss."

"But we still have to get to the consul."

162

The lift stopped. They left it, and walked down the dimly-lit passage to the double doors that led into the street.

"No chances, Harry," Don warned, pausing before the closed doors. "I'll go first. Have your gun handy. Let me get a few yards ahead, then come after me."

Harry nodded.

"Okay, boss."

Don opened one of the doors and peered cautiously out into the dark street.

The few street lamps made isolated pools of light on the pavements, but the rest of the street was shadowy and dark. Any number of people, Don thought, could be lurking in doorways without being seen.

He pulled his gun from his hip-pocket and moved silently from the shelter of the doorway. Keeping close to the wall he went rapidly along the street.

Silhouetted against the night sky, three buildings down the road, he could see a flag-mast with a flag hanging to it, and he guessed that would be the American consulate.

He glanced back over his shoulder. He couldn't see Harry nor hear him, but he guessed he was behind him. He kept on.

Suddenly from a doorway on the other side of the road, Don saw a match flare up as if someone was about to light a cigarette but instead, whoever it was hiding in the darkness, flicked the burning match into the road.

Don realized at once that this must be a signal of some kind. He didn't hesitate. He jumped forward and sprinted down the road towards the consulate. Even as he began to run, he heard a car engine start up and a car come down the road behind him.

He could hear Harry pounding along behind him. The sound of the oncoming car was now ominously near, and he realized it must pass him before he gained the shelter of the consulate.

He looked back over his shoulder.

A big black car without lights was bearing down on him. Suddenly headlights sprang on, and the beams hit him, blinding him and making him lurch against the wall.

Then he heard the sharp crack of Harry's automatic and the sound of glass smashing. The car swerved away and slowed down. Don threw himself flat as a machine-gun opened up from the car.

The dark street was lit up by the yellow flashes from the gun; bullets hammered against the wall of the house before which Don had thrown himself.

Harry's automatic again cracked out. A man yelled in pain, the car suddenly accelerated, and went down the street at high speed and disappeared around the corner.

Don half rose when the bang of a .45 from the doorway across the road where the match lighter had given his signal, made him flatten down again.

A bullet hummed inches past his face, and he fired across the street into the dark doorway.

A man staggered out into the light of the street lamp, bent double, took three tottering steps forward, then dropped face down in the road.

Don jumped to his feet as Harry joined him, and together they raced the intervening yards to the consulate.

As they reached the flight of steps leading to the building, the double doors opened and two American Service cops came out, guns in hand.

Don pulled up sharply and raised his hands above his head. Harry followed suit. Don wasn't taking any chances of being shot by excited and over-enthusiastic cops.

The two policemen approached them warily.

"What's going on around here?" one of them demanded.

Don laughed.

The banal question delivered in a heavy American accent was music to his ears.

"I have urgent business with the consul," he said, stressing his own slight accent. "That was an attempt to kill me you just heard, and if we don't get under cover pretty quick, they'll try again."

"You American?" the cop asked, peering at him.

"My name's Micklem; Don Micklem."

"That's right. I know him," the second cop said. "I've seen his picture in the papers."

Still keeping both Don and Harry covered, the two policemen shepherded them into the safety of the consulate.

# CHAPTER FOURTEEN

*Checkmate*

IN one of the consulate's cars, with an armed Service policeman sitting beside the driver, and with an escort of two motor-cycle cops, Don and Harry were driven rapidly to the Zurich airport.

Edward Jepson, the consul, had acted promptly. The machine-gun attack outside the consulate had aroused his anger, and the attack did more to help Don's cause than any guarded explanation he could give.

He had explained briefly that he was attempting to complete a vitally important mission for the British government, and it was essential to get the oilskin package back to London safely and at once.

Jepson had agreed to send the package by diplomatic bag. He had also agreed to deal personally with the package, and not to delegate the sending of it to any of his secretaries.

Don had told him there was a strong possibility of another attack being made on him at the airport, and Jepson had taken prompt steps by calling for a car and an escort.

"I think we're going to get away with it," Don said as he spotted the distant lights of the airport ahead of them. "All we must hope now is they don't smuggle a bomb on the plane."

"Cheer up, boss," Harry said. "I was just thinking how nice it'll be to get home again."

"I shan't relax until I get rid of the book," Don returned. "Well, here we are. It's all laid on. Jepson called the airport and fixed the tickets. All we have to do is get on board the plane."

"And wait to be blown up," Harry said wryly.

The guard got out of the car as it stopped outside the reception office.

"Hold on a moment, sir," he said. "I'll find out where the plane is."

The other two guards had put up their motor-cycles, and they now stood either side of the car.

"Makes one feel important, doesn't it?" Harry whispered. "All the same I'd as soon look after myself."

"There's nothing to stop you. Keep your eyes skinned."

There was a short wait, then the guard came out of the reception office.

"Here are your tickets, sir," he said, handing two folders to Don. "You have ten minutes to wait. The plane's at Bay Five. We'll drive over there. I've orders to search the plane, but that won't take long."

"Make a job of it," Harry said. "We're not in all that much of a hurry."

The guard got into the car, and they drove rapidly under the bright arc lights that lit up the tarmac to a reception hut before which five other passengers were waiting.

The car swept around the back of the hut and pulled up outside a door.

"If you'll get under cover, sir, I'll call you when we are ready," the guard said as he got out of the car. "We shouldn't be long."

Don and Harry got out of the car, crossed the concrete path and the guard opened the door.

They walked into the small waiting-room and the guard closed the door behind them.

"We could be royalty, couldn't we?" Harry said, going across to an easy chair and sinking into it with a sigh. "We should have gone to one of your consuls before, boss."

Don had crossed to the window and was looking out into the dark night.

"Better keep away from the window," Harry said, then stiffened as he saw the door opposite to the one they had entered open abruptly. Standing in the doorway was Carl Natzka, a .45 in his hand. "Blimey! Where did you spring from?"

"If either of you move, I'll kill you!" Natzka said.

Don turned quickly, his heart skipping a beat.

Natzka moved into the room and Maria followed him in.

"So we meet again, Don," she said gaily. "How nice!"

She was wearing a three-quarter length mink coat over a yellow silk blouse and a black skirt. She came over and sat on the couch and smiled at Don.

"Hello," Don said, and he had to make an effort to keep his face expressionless. He was acutely aware of the leather-bound book in his pocket. "You've mistimed your entrance. There's a guard outside and there are two more within reach."

"The guard outside is in my pay," Natzka said. "Give me the book and you are free to leave on the plane. If you refuse, I will kill you!"

"You don't imagine you could get out of the airport if you did," Don said. "You don't kid me you have all the airport guards in your pay."

Natzka's eyes glittered.

"I would have time to destroy the book. This is all I care about. Hand it over at once!"

"Please give it to him, Don," Maria said earnestly. "He means what he says. Don't be a hero. Give it to him and go free."

Don smiled at her.

"I might be tempted to follow your advice," he said lightly, "but I haven't got the book."

"You can't bluff me!" Natzka snapped. "I'll give you ten seconds to hand it over, and then I'll shoot!"

Looking at him, Don realized he would shoot.

"I took the precaution of giving the book to the consul," he lied. "He is having it flown to London in the diplomatic bag."

"You're lying!"

Don came casually from the window and sat on the couch beside Maria.

"I tell you I haven't got it. It's already in the diplomatic bag. You can search us if you don't believe me."

"I will search you," Natzka snarled, his face white and strained.

Without taking his eyes off them, he opened the door and called, "Busso, come in here."

Don touched Maria's coat sleeve.

"That's a lovely coat." He lifted her wrist and stroked the fur. "Mink makes ugly women attractive, and lovely ones dazzling. I'm dazzled."

Maria looked at him.

"You haven't got it then?" she said. "I thought you would be too clever to be caught so easily."

"I rather expected trouble at the airport," Don returned. "The diplomatic bag seemed the safest bet."

Busso came in and glowered at Don.

"Search these two!" Natzka said. "You know what we're looking for. Be quick!"

"Don't start anything, Harry," Don said mildly and stood up, raising his hands.

Harry watched with popping eyes.

Busso ran his hands over Don, then stepped away. He looked at Natzka.

"Nothing, signore."

"The other man!" Natzka rapped out.

"Let him do it," Don said as Harry got to his feet.

"Anything you say, boss," Harry said blankly.

Again Busso ran his hands expertly over Harry and again shook his head.

"Now are you satisfied?" Don said, sitting down again beside Maria. "You're beaten. No one can get at the bag. It leaves to-night under armed escort."

"You are stupid to tell me about the bag," Natzka said, his eyes burning feverishly. He motioned to Busso who pulled out a gun and covered Don and Harry. Then Natzka went over to the telephone standing on the table.

"Give me the American consulate," he said into the mouthpiece. There was a pause, then he said, "Give me Mr. Channing." Another pause. "Channing? A small package, done up in green oilskin, was handed to the consul less than half an hour ago. It is to be put in a diplomatic bag and flown to London to-night. I want it. You understand? Get it and bring it to me at the usual place. You will not return to the consulate. Your work is finished here." He listened for a moment, then said, "Good. I'll expect you in half an hour," and he hung up. He turned and looked at Don, his eyes triumphant. "It seems I win after all, Mr. Micklem. My man tells me he will have no difficulty in getting at the bag."

Don knew he would have to play the farce out to the end. Natzka must not suspect for a moment he had been tricked.

"Why, you treacherous rat!" he exploded. "Don't imagine you're going to get away with this!"

Natzka laughed.

"Come, Mr. Micklem, there's no need to lose your temper. An individual can never beat an organization. You had a good try and you gave me several unpleasant moments. After all, this matter has nothing to do with your country."

Don pretended to swallow his anger. He shrugged.

"Well, okay, you win."

"That's more like it," Natzka said. "All the same, I will admit I shall be glad to see the last of you. You have been very persistent. Busso will see you on to the plane. By the time you reach Paris I shall be out of reach. If you attempt to elude Busso, he will shoot you. I have no intentions of giving you a chance to stir up more trouble." He looked at Busso. "Take them to the plane. If they make a false move, shoot them!"

"Come," Busso said, going to the door.

Don turned to Maria.

"So it's goodbye. I had hoped you might be forced to seek sanctuary in England. I would like to have shown you the English historic places of interest. I know London as well as I know Venice."

Out of the corner of his eye he saw Natzka leave the room. Maria got to her feet. She was smiling.

"Perhaps one day I will come to England," she said. "I will remember the invitation."

"Come!" Busso snarled.

Don ignored him.

"Have you to run after your brother?" he asked her. "Or will you come to the plane and see me off?"

"Do you want me to?"

"Yes. Call me sentimental if you like, but a beautiful woman waving goodbye is always a pleasant memory."

Her eyes sparkled and she laughed.

"You shall have your memory."

Don linked his arm in hers.

"Then let's go."

He walked to the door, followed by Harry who was looking uneasily at Don, puzzled the book wasn't found on Don, and disapproving of his friendliness with Maria.

Busso brought up the rear.

As they crossed to where the aircraft was warming up, Don said, "Why don't you come with me, Maria? Why don't you settle in London?"

"Why should I? What has London to offer? Besides, I couldn't desert Carl; he relies on me so much."

"I am thinking of your safety. Sooner or later, you are going to regret working with him."

"I never have any regrets."

A pretty air-hostess, looking worried, ran up.

"Mr. Micklem?"

"Yes."

"We've been waiting for you. Will you please get on board immediately?"

"I'm sorry. I'll be right with you. Go ahead, Harry," Don said, turning to Harry, and Harry again looking at him uneasily, ran up the portable staircase and into the aircraft.

Don turned to face Maria.

"Goodbye and good luck."

"You said that before."

"I say it again." He put his arm round her; his other hand slid down the arm of her coat. "You and mink: a lovely combination." He kissed her lightly. "Sure you won't come with me?"

She shook her head.

"Goodbye, Don."

He turned and ran up the staircase, paused to wave to her, then ducked into the aircraft.

The door closed and the staircase was run away.

Don sank into the seat beside Harry.

The aircraft engines roared and the machine began to move towards the runway.

Don looked through the window and again waved to Maria as she stood under an arc light waving back to him.

Then when the aircraft began its steady climb, Don turned to look at Harry.

"Phew!" he said. "Those last few moments put years on my life."

"I noticed that, boss," Harry said stiffly.

Don smiled and half-turning so the other passengers couldn't see, he showed Harry the leather-bound book he held in his hand.

"I slipped it in the turn-up of her cuff before Busso searched me," he said, keeping his voice down. "She carried it to the aircraft for us."

"Well, I'll be blowed!" Harry said, and his disapproving face lit up with a delighted grin.

Two and a half hours later, the aircraft touched down on the Northolt runway and the journey was over.

Don had realized that it wouldn't have taken long for Natzka to find out he had been tricked. There was a chance that he had been able to get into touch with his agents in London and they would make an attempt to get the book before it was handed to Sir Robert Graham.

Leaving nothing to chance, Don had persuaded the captain of the aircraft to send a signal to Sir Robert asking him to arrange to have the plane met by a police escort.

As the plane came to a standstill, Don said, "Let the other passengers get out first. Have your gun ready, Harry."

Harry nodded.

Don had told the air-hostess there might be trouble when

they landed, and she stood by the aircraft door until the last of the passengers had alighted.

"Go to her, Harry," Don said. "Take a look outside."

Harry went to the door.

"Okay, miss, you buzz off," he said cheerfully. "You can leave this to me."

The girl, a little flustered, descended the staircase to the ground.

Coming across the tarmac Harry saw a small group of men, headed by a tall, dignified man with white drooping moustaches.

"It's okay, boss," Harry said. "Here's Super. Tom Dicks and an old cove who looks like Sir Robert."

Don joined him at the door.

Chief Superintendent Tom Dicks, placidly smoking a pipe, waved to him. Sir Robert raised his stick in greeting.

Don descended the staircase and shook hands with Sir Robert and then with Dicks.

"What have you been up to, my boy?" Sir Robert demanded, looking keenly at him.

"I've been hunting for Tregarth," Don said quietly. "He gave me something for you and I'll be glad to be relieved of the responsibility of it." He took the book from his pocket and handed it to Sir Robert.

"What is it?" Sir Robert asked sharply.

"Something Tregarth said you must have at all costs," Don returned. "I don't know what it is, but he lost his life trying to get it to you."

"Lost his life?" Sir Robert's eyes hardened. "They killed him then?"

"Yes, they killed him."

"The car's waiting, Sir Robert," Dicks said. "No point hanging around here. It's too exposed for my liking."

"Yes, you're quite right," Sir Robert said and handed Dicks the leather-bound book. "Here, you take charge of it."

"Don't lose it, Super," Don said. "They may still be after it."

Dicks smiled grimly.

"I'd like to see them try and get it," he said, dropping the book in his pocket. "I'll take it to Colonel Henderson, Sir Robert. We'll telephone you as soon as we know." He looked at Don and gave him his wide, placid smile. "It would seem it is sometimes a good thing when some people don't mind their own business, Mr. Micklem. Good night," and he walked off, followed by two burly plain-clothes men.

Sir Robert said, "I have my car here, Don. Come home with me. I want to talk to you."

With Harry sitting next to the chauffeur, Sir Robert and Don settled down at the back of the Daimler that was waiting at the reception hut.

The car drove out on to Western Avenue and began its journey to London.

"So you found Tregarth," Sir Robert said, offering his cigar-case. "These are not as good as yours, my boy, but they'll do."

"Yes, I found him," Don said. He struck a match and lit the cigar.

"You're an obstinate young devil," Sir Robert said, shaking his head. "You could have ruined everything. I told you to keep out of this business."

"You wouldn't have got what you have got if I had kept out," Don returned.

"Yes, that's true," Sir Robert said and frowned at the glowing end of his cigar. "It wasn't a good plan, but it was a gamble that might have come off. Poor Tregarth was so enthusiastic and sure he persuaded me to let him go. The weakness was that he had to act alone. He was so sure he could beat them."

"You forget I don't know the background, and I think I'm entitled to know."

Sir Robert nodded.

"I'll tell you some of it, but not here. Wait until we get home. Suppose you tell me what's been happening? I'll want a written report from you for Colonel Henderson, but give me some details now."

Until they reached Sir Robert's Kensington home, Don recounted in detail what had happened in Venice. He had just concluded when the car pulled up outside Sir Robert's home.

"'Pon my soul!" Sir Robert said. "It's a fantastic story." He climbed stiffly out on to the pavement. "Well, come in. Jedson, look after Mr. Micklem's man. Give him something to eat and a whisky. I've no doubt he deserves it."

Jedson, Sir Robert's chauffeur, touched his cap. His face brightened considerably. He could see no reason why Harry should drink on his own.

Leaving Harry and Jedson together, Sir Robert opened the front door, handed his hat, coat and stick to his butler and led

Don into a big, comfortably-furnished study, walled with books, with a bright fire burning in the grate.

"Sit down, Don," Sir Robert said, and went over to the liquor cabinet. "Will you have a brandy? I've got some good stuff here. Not many bottles left now unfortunately. Came from my father's cellar."

"I'd rather have a whisky," Don said, sitting down before the fire.

"Hmm. When I was a boy, brandy was considered the thing to drink after midnight. Well, never mind..." Sir Robert brought a glass of whisky and water and set it on the table by Don's side. He sat down, holding a balloon glass with brandy in it between his thin, veined hands.

"Yes, that's a fantastic story," he said, picking up the threads where Don had left off. "I know Natzka's reputation well. He's dangerous and clever. You did well to beat him." He looked across at Don. "Well, my boy, I'll tell you a little of my side of the story, but it mustn't go further. You understand?"

Don nodded.

"About nine months ago, we became aware of a bad leak in information to do with – well, perhaps that doesn't matter," Sir Robert said, frowning down at his brandy. "The less you know about the details the better. Anyway, someone was giving away important information; someone who must have been in a high position. It made things extremely awkward. It got so bad the heads of the various departments began to suspect each other. I daresay some of the fools even suspected me." He sipped a little of his brandy, and nodded approvingly. "Sure you won't change your mind, my boy? This is really a splendid brandy."

"No, thank you," Don said. "Where does Tregarth fit into this?"

"Yes, Tregarth." Sir Robert shook his head. "Poor fellow! We shall miss him. He was easily our best agent. He had the courage of a lion. Things got so bad; so much vital information was leaking over to the other side that I decided to consult him. Set a thief to catch a thief – you understand? Nobody had any ideas who could be behind the leak, and I thought he might have a bright suggestion. Well, he had. We did know that the information was finding its way into Natzka's hands. Tregarth suggested he should pretend to go over to the other side, win Natzka's confidence and try to find out from Natzka's end who the man was who was giving the information away." Sir Robert got up to poke the fire which didn't need poking. "I thought

173

the idea was too dangerous. I could see they might accept Tregarth as a traitor, especially if we played our parts well here. I could see, too, that he might even get the information for us, but I couldn't see how he could get back alive. I told him so, but he said he was ready to take the risk." The old man crossed his thin legs and stared doubtfully at Don, his big, moist eyes reminding Don of the eyes of a codfish. "You've met his wife?"

"Yes," Don said. "I've met her."

"A nice, sensible girl; not like most of the dolly-mops you see about these days. Well, I thought of her, Don. I told Tregarth it wasn't fair on her. I shan't forget in a hurry what he said." Sir Robert drank some more brandy. "The boy said, 'This isn't the time for sentiment. There's a job to be done and I'm going to do it. I'll trouble you, sir, not to worry about my wife. She's my affair.' This isn't the time for sentiment. Hmm, well, it wasn't, but I was pretty sure he was throwing away his life, and I felt . . . Well, never mind. He went. Since the man we were after could have access to any papers coming into my office, it was essential to convince him, whoever he was, that Tregarth had turned traitor. We did it so well and Tregarth played his part so efficiently, he was accepted by Natzka. We got one radio message from him. It was brief, but to the point. He said he had got Natzka's list of agents operating in this country. The list was in code and he couldn't crack the code. He said he would do his best to get it to me. Well, he did the next best thing. He gave it to you to give to me."

"Will you crack the code?" Don asked.

Sir Robert shrugged.

"It may not be necessary. You can be sure this spy has been warned. He may try and bolt and we'll have him."

Don finished his whisky and got to his feet.

"Thank you for putting me in the picture, Sir Robert. Now, I must run; I have something that won't wait to do."

Sir Robert blinked at him.

"My dear boy, I was hoping you'd stay the night here. After all, you've had a very exhausting time. Your house is shut up, isn't it?"

"I've got Harry. He can take care of the house, and I can take care of myself. I'll let you have a written report in a day or so. Right now I have something to take care of."

"Well, all right." Sir Robert went to the door and told the butler to fetch Harry. As he came back into the room, the telephone bell rang.

"Excuse me a moment. That might be Dicks," he said, and picked up the receiver. He listened to the voice that growled against his ear. "'Pon my soul!" he exclaimed suddenly. "I'd better come down. You don't think it necessary? Well, all right. Come and see me when you have a moment, Colonel. Yes, yes; we won't tell the press too much. A nervous breakdown or something like that. No doubt someone will want to ask a question in the house, but we can put a stopper on him. I'll wait for you," and hung up.

He stood pulling at his moustache, his face grave. Then he glanced up and caught Don's eye.

"One of my colleagues has just shot himself. A man whom I trusted." He stared at Don, then lifted his shoulders. "Tregarth didn't die for nothing."

"No," Don said. "Well, good night, Sir Robert."

"Where are you going, my boy?" Sir Robert asked as he shook hands.

"I'm going to see Tregarth's wife."

"At this hour? It's getting on for two. You shouldn't disturb her now."

"I shan't disturb her. Can I borrow your car?"

"By all means. Do you want my man?"

"Harry will drive."

"Ah, yes. But don't you think you'd better wait until the morning? She'll be sleeping."

Don shook his head.

"If I were waiting news of someone I loved as much as Hilda Tregarth loves her husband, I don't think I'd sleep much. Good night, Sir Robert."

Calling to Harry, Don went down the steps into the dark night.